Change of
the Heart

Also by Lynn Bulock
in Large Print:

Heart Games
The Promise of Summer

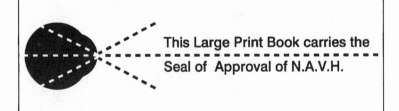

This Large Print Book carries the
Seal of Approval of N.A.V.H.

Change of the Heart

Lynn Bulock

Thorndike Press • Waterville, Maine

Published in 2003 by arrangement with Harlequin Books S.A.

Thorndike Press® Large Print Christian Romance.

The tree indicium is a trademark of Thorndike Press.

The text of this Large Print edition is unabridged.
Other aspects of the book may vary from the original edition.

Set in 16 pt. Plantin.

Printed in the United States on permanent paper.

Library of Congress Cataloging-in-Publication Data

Bulock, Lynn.
     Change of the heart / Lynn Bulock.
        p. cm.
     ISBN 0-7862-5760-1 (lg. print : hc : alk. paper)
     1. Church work with teenagers — Fiction. 2. Physicians
— Fiction. 3. Large type books. I. Title.
PS3552.U463C47 2003
     813′.54—dc21   2003054247

To Joe, always
And to my critique partners
Luanne, Natalie and Annie . . .
you keep me sane!

As the Founder/CEO of NAVH, the only national health agency solely devoted to those who, although not totally blind, have an eye disease which could lead to serious visual impairment, I am pleased to recognize Thorndike Press★ as one of the leading publishers in the large print field.

Founded in 1954 in San Francisco to prepare large print textbooks for partially seeing children, NAVH became the pioneer and standard setting agency in the preparation of large type.

Today, those publishers who meet our standards carry the prestigious "Seal of Approval" indicating high quality large print. We are delighted that Thorndike Press is one of the publishers whose titles meet these standards. We are also pleased to recognize the significant contribution Thorndike Press is making in this important and growing field.

Lorraine H. Marchi, L.H.D.
Founder/CEO
NAVH

★ Thorndike Press encompasses the following imprints: Thorndike, Wheeler, Walker and Large Pr int Press.

You are all children of God through faith in Christ Jesus, for all of you who were baptized into Christ have clothed yourselves with Christ. There is neither Jew nor Greek, slave nor free, male nor female, for you are all one in Christ Jesus.

— *Galatians* 3:26–28

Chapter One

"Are you sure we need to do this?" Carrie Collins asked her friend Elaine as they bounced around in an ambulance on a rough county road. Carrie Collins didn't usually put much stock in April Fools' Day. And if anyone had told her that this year her least favorite holiday would change her life forever, she would have considered it the ultimate April Fools' joke.

Carrie liked a good, harmless practical joke as much as the next person. She'd participated in her share of them in the five years she'd been with the county Fire and Rescue squad. But the day started so uneventfully it was hard to believe everything might change. She worked her normal shift, changed into shorts and a T-shirt and went over to the high school gym to lead the Fire and Rescue coed team to victory in their volleyball league, or so she thought.

One minute she missed an easy dive and

the next minute she was sitting in the wrong end of one of her own ambulances. "I'm positive you need to do this. The patient's point of view isn't nearly as much fun, is it?" Elaine said. Carrie winced because her wrist hurt and Elaine was right. Riding in an ambulance as a patient was *not* fun. She'd take her field supervisor's position any day.

Carrie's wrist began to throb, and every bounce of the rig made it feel even worse. "Still think it's just sprained?" Elaine, her friend and paramedic, asked with a smirk.

"I certainly do." Her wrist had to be just sprained. A break would keep her out of work for weeks, and she had no desire to sit around her apartment and contemplate the walls. Besides, she just wasn't meant to sit still. Four or more weeks off duty and she'd be ready for the funny farm.

The ambulance stopped, and Elaine headed for the back doors. "You *will* let me open up, help you down and get you in there, understand?" Carrie took offense at her tone. Elaine sounded like a mother addressing a stubborn toddler. She felt at least eleven right now, certainly no toddler.

"Fine. Open the doors and help me down if it makes you feel better." Carrie sucked in her breath quickly when her feet made contact with the pavement.

"You okay? Not going to pass out on me or anything?" Elaine looked concerned now.

"Never. I'm tougher than that." Just barely, Carrie told herself, sending up a silent prayer to stay upright while the doors to the emergency room whooshed open.

Sue, the trauma nurse who was in charge of triage at Washington General most days, scrunched up her face when she saw Carrie. "I don't like the looks of this."

"Yeah, well neither do I," Carrie shot back. "It'll teach me to worry about tripping over my partner on the volleyball court."

Sue balled up her fists on her hips. "So you didn't even do this on the job? You were playing volleyball?" She led Carrie over to a chair and looked her over. "I should have figured that out. You don't wear grubby shorts and a jersey to work." She pulled a moistened wipe out of a nearby container and swiped Carrie's face.

"Thanks," Carrie told her, but she knew Sue's gesture had less to do with kindness and more to do with assessing Carrie's skin color. It was hard to gauge if somebody was about to keel over when she had a huge smudge of sweaty dirt on her cheek.

"Any time. Now try to be a good patient, because we're busy tonight and it may be a while."

Carrie groaned inwardly, but nodded and sat, cradling her wrist. It was beginning to throb and swell some more. Sue finished the rest of her intake procedure and waved Carrie over to another window, where a kid barely out of his teens took her insurance number and personal information. After that, Carrie insisted that Elaine and her crew go back to the rig to write up their report and leave.

"You don't mind being left here by yourself?"

"Oh, don't go all mother hen on me, Elaine," Carrie snapped. "You wouldn't stay for anybody else you brought in with a sprain, or even a break. There are worse situations out there for you to take care of. Go do it. I'll get a ride home when I'm done."

Carrie said goodbye to Elaine and the ambulance driver and went back to the paperwork she had to fill out to get treated. It wasn't easy with her right wrist in this much pain.

Once she was done signing everything for the insurance company, she walked slowly over to the waiting room to look for a seat on the worn vinyl furniture.

It wasn't an easy task. The walk itself jarred her wrist again, and there was little space once she made it to the waiting area. The one television was tuned to some sitcom she wouldn't have watched at home under any conditions. Several toddlers and grade-school-age kids seemed to be watching the program once in a while between running around the room or tossing the ancient magazines at each other.

Every few minutes Sue would call another name and an individual or a family would disappear through the double doors into the treatment area. Carrie thought about calling one of her sisters to come sit with her, but dismissed the idea pretty quickly.

They were both busy with their families and demanding jobs, and by early evening would be cooking dinner or trying to relax at home. No sense dragging Claire or Laurel to an emergency room.

At least having a suspected break gave her a change of scenery while she waited. Sue shuffled her down a side hall to radiology, where a young, harried technician took films of her wrist, apologizing for any pain he caused her. He was good at his job and there was little pain involved. When Carrie told him that he smiled, as if few people bothered to compliment him on his work. Then she went back to the waiting room while they got her films together.

Finally, nearly two hours after she'd come into the E.R., Carrie's name was called. "Thanks for being a good sport," Sue said, motioning her into a curtained cubicle. "We are so shorthanded tonight. Dr. O'Connor will be in as soon as he can."

O'Connor wasn't a name Carrie recognized, but the emergency room slots turned over more quickly than other jobs at Washington General. Trauma teams tended to be filled with young people who spent a few years on the job, then went someplace more exciting than the cluster of small towns here in eastern Missouri. Or they just burned out on the demanding job and left for something less exciting than emergency work.

She looked down at her wrist. No matter how badly she wanted it to be just sprained, she was beginning to admit to herself that it looked broken. It felt just dandy, too. While she examined it gingerly, a head popped into the break in the curtains shielding her from the other cubicles. "Hi. Let me get my intern and I'll be back in a minute."

Before Carrie could react, the man was gone. If that was Dr. O'Connor, his bedside manner could use some work. She hadn't gotten much more than a blurred glance at him before he disappeared in a flurry of white coat.

He was back in a moment, or at least somebody in a white coat was back. It was probably the same man who had popped in the first time. This person was fairly young and dark-haired, and strode into the room quickly. He had a very young-looking woman with him and before she got all the way into the cubicle, he was briskly putting Carrie's X rays up on the light board on the wall. "Classic Colles' fracture," he said with a smug, satisfied tone Carrie took offense to right away. "See it, Jan? Right there."

"Uh, hello? Would you be Dr. O'Connor?" Carrie said, aware that her voice was colder than the chilled air in the bay around them.

"I would. And you are . . ." He paused, looking down at the envelope that held her X rays a moment before. "Carolyn. Is your mom or dad here, Carolyn, so we can talk to them?"

"It's Carrie. Or Ms. Collins. And no, they're not here. Just how old do you think I am?" Carrie felt her voice rising in anger. "Do you treat all your patients this rudely, Dr. O'Connor?"

He had the good grace to blush a little, suffusing his tanned cheeks with an even deeper glow. Carrie had to admit he was a very handsome man. Too bad they'd met under these circumstances instead. "No. I'm sorry, Ms. Collins. I saw the sports uniform and the ponytail and I made an assumption. Most of the sports injuries tonight have been high school kids, and I guess I just figured that you were, too."

"Well, I'm not."

"No, I can see that now. Quite clearly." His intense assessment of her made Carrie want to squirm on the gurney.

A flash of aggravation replaced her discomfort almost immediately. "If I were a kid like you first thought, I'd be scared to death by the way you barged in here. You told a total stranger that my wrist was broken, without ever saying a word to me." Carrie found it awkward to confront the man and hold her damaged wrist at the same time, especially when he kept staring at her with that dark gaze.

16

The doctor sighed and moved toward her. Carrie could see fine lines around his eyes when he got this close. They didn't look like age lines, more like fatigue. "Look, I said I was sorry. You're about the fortieth patient I've seen in a tight twelve-hour shift. I haven't been off the floor since lunch. That was eleven this morning, and lasted fifteen minutes before I got paged. And Jan here is doing her first rotation in the emergency room and I'm trying to get her up to speed as quickly as possible."

Dr. O'Connor looked contrite close up. His eyes were even darker than his cocoa-colored hair, and his lean cheeks and high cheekbones gave Carrie the impression he'd be more at home with a cowboy hat on his head than a stethoscope around his neck.

Yes, he definitely looked like a cowboy. Carrie dropped her gaze to check out his shoes. The boots weren't snakeskin, just battered cowhide. They poked out from under jeans that looked like they'd seen plenty of hard work.

The frayed hems and worn boots made Carrie more sympathetic to the man. Since she'd heard his explanation, she had to admit she knew exactly what Dr. O'Connor was feeling. Stress and lack of rest didn't make for the best attitude.

"Okay, Dr. O'Connor, I'll cut you a break. But next time I'm on the other end of the process and bringing you in a real injured teenager, be nicer to them than you were to me, okay?"

O'Connor looked down at the clipboard that held her information. "Is that what you do when you're not visiting emergency rooms? You visit other emergency rooms?"

"That about covers it. I'm a field supervisor for Fire and Rescue in Friedens. Which means I don't ride rigs all the time, and Washington General isn't our first hospital of choice for anything but serious trauma, but yes, you're likely to see me in uniform."

"Then I'll definitely be nice to you, and any teenagers you bring in. I get along much better with real teenagers. That should have tipped me off that you were older," he shot back. Carrie heard the intern stifle a laugh.

She was forcing back a smile herself. "Just spare me the explanations and get the splint for this classic fracture, okay?"

O'Connor's straight dark brows pulled together. "Splint? I don't think so. Not on that wrist."

Carrie felt her temper rising again.

"Come on. I've been working Fire and Rescue for years. And if this is a Colles' fracture, like you said, you can splint it and I can be on my way."

"So you can take the splint off the first time it bothers you? Not on your life."

"Who are you to make that call?"

"Your attending physician, Ms. Collins. If you'd like me to get some backup, I'll be happy to do so. The only orthopedic specialist on duty tonight normally works in pediatrics, but in this case his opinion might be welcome."

Carrie restrained herself from sticking her tongue out at him since that would have made O'Connor's point. "Fine. Whatever. But if you cast it I'll be out of work for weeks."

The doctor rolled his expressive brown eyes. "That's the general idea. If you use this wrist too much, you're going to aggravate the fracture instead of letting it heal properly. Not only will it take longer, but twenty years from now you'll be calling me all kinds of names when arthritis settles into the joint."

Carrie took a deep breath. He had a point. Six weeks of boredom now might be worth better use of her wrist later on. And she *would* take a splint off if it got aggravating. But why did this cocky emergency room doctor have to be right? He looked like a man used to getting his way.

"Just give me something for pain and set this thing before I get any crankier. Will your pediatric friend give me a balloon when I'm done?"

His answering smile was brilliant. "Only if you let him tie it to your wrist. You look like the kind that would cry when you lost it."

Rafe O'Connor watched the orthopedic specialist put the finishing touches on Carolyn Collins's cast. He still thought he wasn't far off thinking she was a high schooler. That youthful disposition along with her cutoff jeans and a baggy athletic shirt would have made anybody think they were dealing with a kid.

But on closer look, her blue eyes had a wit and sparkle most of his younger friends lacked because they didn't have the life experience most adults did. Though at first glance the bright red ponytail took a few years off her age.

But if he really assessed the woman before him, it was easy to see that she was probably in her middle to late twenties. And very attractive. If he weren't so dead on his feet he'd see if she wanted to grab something to eat in the cafeteria and let him sign her cast. Maybe he'd even leave his phone number on it. . . .

Rafe shook his head to clear the cobwebs. Now he knew he'd really been working for way too long without a break. Flirting with a patient? It was so far from his normal behavior that it shocked him.

Not only was Ms. Collins a patient, but according to what she'd told him she was almost a co-worker, as well. True, from what he'd overheard her tell the orthopedic guy, she didn't spend most of her time riding the rigs for Fire and Rescue. Still, it was likely she'd be transporting patients in and out of his emergency room once she got back on the job. Even the investigators, which she admitted to being, got their share of runs on a service as small as that of Friedens.

"Carolyn? Is somebody waiting for you?" Rafe blurted, grabbing her attention from the orthopedist who was giving her instructions.

"It's Carrie. Nobody calls me Carolyn. No, no one's waiting on me, at least not yet. I figured I'd give one of my sisters a call, or my dad."

"So no husband or roommate or anything?" Suddenly her answer seemed very important to Rafe. The casted hand was bare of rings, but it was her right hand. Without being too obvious, he tried to glance at her other hand for any significant jewelry.

"No, nobody but me and the goldfish in the apartment. And the goldfish are the plastic kind because I'm real bad about feeding live ones." She smiled, and it lit up her face. She really did look like a high schooler, especially with the light freckles dusting her nose and cheeks.

There was a smudge on her cheek, and Rafe had to force himself not to use the hem of his white coat to clear the dirt off her smooth skin. "Well, you can't call a plastic goldfish to pick you up. Will someone be willing to drive you home?"

Carrie nodded. "I appreciate your concern, Dr. O'Connor. I'm sure some of my family will be happy to come get me."

It was a clear tone of dismissal. "Okay. Well, pay attention to what Sam tells you. And don't even think about removing the cast or reaching down there with a knitting needle or something when it itches."

"And it will itch," she said with a sigh. "I'll remember you when I'm sitting around with nothing to keep my mind off that for the next six weeks, Dr. O'Connor."

"I don't doubt that." Rafe turned to Dr. Sam Taylor. "Are you sure six weeks will be enough? Should you make it eight to make sure she doesn't reinjure the area?"

"Eight weeks? You can't be serious. O'Connor, get back in here!" The noises Carrie Collins was making as he left the room were indescribable. Rafe was sure that if her throwing hand hadn't been busy, some nearby object, like Sam's clipboard, would have come sailing out of the cubicle at his head.

He almost wished she'd tried it. He would have liked an excuse to spend a little more time with the intriguing and aggravating Carrie Collins. Not that he had any time for either aggravation or intrigue in his life right now. But if he had, a feisty woman like Carrie would be just the kind of woman he'd look for.

Chapter Two

Carrie wondered which one of her sisters she should call from the emergency room. Even though she'd assured the rather smug E.R. doctor that she had the situation under control, she wasn't so sure she did. She knew what she wasn't going to do. She wasn't about to call her dad — just six months after recovery from heart surgery — to come and get her. She figured he'd done his time in the E.R. So which sister did she call?

Claire was more likely to be home, but might give her a lecture about diving on the volleyball court. Her oldest sister, Laurel, didn't know enough about volleyball to question her judgment, but was still technically a newlywed and more than likely was busy with something, anyway.

Finally Carrie decided to call Laurel first, then Claire if nobody answered at Laurel and Jesse's house. That turned out to be the right decision because everybody seemed to be home at the Jordan and Harrison household. Carrie got offers for a ride home from her brother-in-law Jesse, any squad car from his county sheriff's department that was in the area, or Laurel herself.

She would have chosen an anonymous police cruiser, but none of Jesse's officers were in the next county where the hospital was located. So Carrie settled down to wait the twenty minutes or so for her sister to drive to Washington General Hospital and get her.

"Thanks. I really appreciate this," she told Laurel as she got into her car in the emergency room parking lot. Just opening the door and getting in was awkward with a cast on her right arm. Carrie thought for a moment that maybe she should have taken the sling the doctors offered. But that would have made things even more awkward.

"You can thank me later. I've got ideas on how you could repay me and you may not like any of them." Laurel smiled so that her eyes crinkled, and looked over at Carrie in the passenger seat. "Do we need to stop at a pharmacy anyplace? I seem to remember from Jeremy's bouts with broken bones that other goodies are required, like pain pills and slings and such."

That was the problem with her older sisters. They knew how patients were supposed to behave because their husbands and teenage kids had given them plenty of opportunities to nurse them back to health. Carrie shook her head, then realized Laurel couldn't see her in the dark. "I'm good, really. They didn't prescribe anything stronger for pain than I've got at home in the medicine chest. And I'm holding off on the sling until I see what my work situation is going to be."

Laurel snorted. "Work situation? You don't think they're going to let you work with that cast on, do you? I'm pretty sure Dad would blow a gasket if he found out." Their father, the county sheriff before Jesse had taken over the job, still had enough sway with the rest of the county officials to convince Carrie Laurel was right.

"And he has to know about this because . . . ?" Carrie said, with more bravado than she actually felt.

"Because he's still your father, even if you are a grown-up. And I think the grown-up part is debatable if you're really thinking of working Fire and Rescue with that thing on your arm."

Carrie attempted a shrug. This seemed to be her day to learn to give in gracefully. "Whatever. I'll let the brass decide tomorrow when I go in. As quickly as the department grapevine works, it won't be any surprise when I show up with a foot of fiberglass on my arm." She leaned back in the car seat. "But what am I going to do if I don't go back to work? I'll go nuts staring at the walls at home in about two days."

It was dark enough outside that Carrie could only see her sister's expression by the glow of headlights passing her vehicle. But she was pretty sure Laurel was smiling in a rather smug fashion. "Oh, we might be able to keep you busy. Come over to the coffeehouse tomorrow after you deal with work. Or you can just stay the night tonight instead of going home alone. . . ."

"No, thanks. Really. I love you and your family all dearly, but I'm ready to crash. Alone, and in relative silence. Which I suspect is something hard to come by in your house."

"You've got me there." Laurel chuckled. "*Peaceful* isn't the best adjective to describe our place. *Happy* almost always works, but *peaceful,* not very often. Too much laughter, noise, teen music and other commotion for peaceful."

Carrie was thankful for her small, quiet and empty apartment that night. Of course getting ready for bed wasn't any picnic with one hand. Why did they make jean shorts so hard to unfasten, anyway? Driving in to work tomorrow was going to be a real challenge, she could already tell. In the end she settled for a bowl of cereal for her late dinner, because the other alternatives she had on hand were microwavable frozen meals, which all seemed to require two hands to open the boxes.

Exhausted and still a little woozy from the pain medication, Carrie slept well. Drifting off, she worried that shifting around with a cast on would wake her up often. But the next time she opened her eyes it was daylight and she'd slept through the night.

One look in the mirror in the morning told Carrie she needed to stop by the hair salon on her way to work. Nobody should try to prove herself fit to hold down a demanding physical job with hair that looked like hers. In fact, nobody with hair that looked like hers should go anywhere without a baseball cap. She never went to a salon for just a shampoo, but this was definitely an emergency.

Even after a shampoo and blow-dry and the fast-food breakfast she treated herself to afterwards, Carrie already knew what the answer was going to be before she walked into the service director's office. She couldn't even get her whole uniform on alone. How could anyone think she was fit for work when she presented herself wearing sweatpants and a T-shirt?

Once she got the official word she was on leave, she stopped by the cubicle she shared with her partner, Rick, when they were in the station. She left him a badly typed note printed out on the computer, letting him know what avoiding stepping on him on the volleyball court had cost her. She added that she would be out for at least six weeks, unless she got pronounced fit for duty sooner.

Carrie felt her anger growing with every passing moment as she left the Fire and Rescue building. She wanted to throw a real tantrum, kick the trash can or something. She had this giant ball of frustration building up inside and no way to release it.

Carrie settled for walking the four blocks to where her sister's coffee shop was located. The Right Place would be open by now, and Laurel would be her obnoxiously cheerful morning self. Carrie knew it would aggravate her more than usual today, but maybe she could drown her sorrows in a white-chocolate mocha and get some sympathy from Laurel at the same time.

Walking through downtown Friedens made part of her foul mood lift. It was a fine spring day and the walk felt good. At least she could walk without being hampered by her cast. By the time the bell jangled over the doorway of The Right Place, Carrie felt a little better. And Laurel didn't even wait to ask what she wanted. Carrie's disappointment at being on leave must have been obvious, because her sister was already putting together her coffee before she reached the counter.

By the time she hoisted herself onto the high stool that didn't seem nearly as comfortable as usual with only one hand to balance herself, Laurel was putting a pale, foamy mocha on the counter, crowned with real whipped cream. "Extra chocolate shavings, too. You look like you need them," her sister said with a grimace. "So, was I right? You're off work?"

"For at least six weeks. Probably more like eight." Carrie bent down to sip the whipped cream and chocolate before she tried to drink any of the coffee. It would be a while before she could drink the steaming liquid without taking the skin off her tongue.

"You're not joining me?" she asked after her first sip. Usually Laurel made herself a mocha to go with Carrie's. It was one of their shared pleasures.

Laurel shook her head. Was her older sister blushing?

"Nope. I've switched over to decaf lattes, heavy on the milk, for a while."

Carrie tried to decipher what her sister was telling her. It seemed to be something momentous, because Laurel's perfectly done cinnamon hair framed a shy smile and sparkling eyes.

Carrie felt denser than usual. What would make Laurel, the family coffee fanatic, stop drinking the stuff? Was it something health related? Suddenly, the simplest, most logical answer made her gasp.

"Oh, wow. You and Jesse are . . . ? Laurel, that is so cool. When are you due?"

"August, by everybody's best count." Laurel was smiling broadly now.

"Okay. Whoa. That will make you . . ." Carrie began.

Laurel finished up for her. "Thirty-seven by the time this kid shows up. I can count."

She put a hand unconsciously high on her still-flat stomach, and her nose wrinkled slightly. "Thanks for reminding me. Older women have done it, you know. In fact, Mom wasn't much younger when you were born, squirt."

Carrie looked at her sister again, feeling a touch of worry. "You're okay? And Jesse and the kids know?"

Laurel smiled, and Carrie felt her worry recede. This was her calm, in-control sister. "Feeling fine, other than that silly complication of being allergic to my toothpaste in the morning. And Jesse and the kids are all thrilled. They all think this is a wonderful thing. So do I most of the time, but it has put a crimp in one thing."

"What's that?" Carrie asked.

Laurel leaned her chin on one palm. "I had already committed to going on the kids' mission trip a couple weeks from now before I found out about our little bundle of joy. And Jesse is having fits at the thought of me in Tijuana for any length of time, even for a week."

"Tijuana? As in Mexico? That sounds pretty cool," Carrie said, finally taking a healthy swallow of her cooling mocha. "I can see where you wouldn't want to miss that."

"Not at all. Even the camping part sounded pretty good when their youth minister talked about it. Apparently Rafe has done this before, and he makes it sound like the adventure of a lifetime. Jeremy and Ashleigh are both signed up to go."

"Will your not being able to go be a problem for them? Can they still make the trip?"

Laurel shrugged. "I guess. Rafe's pretty strict about taking adequate numbers of adult sponsors on trips with the high school youth. And I'm almost sure from what he told me that I have to go, or somebody has to go in my place, for this trip to work. If not, I know my kids would be the first to be put on the waiting list if he's shorthanded."

Laurel looked pointedly at her sister, and Carrie felt awareness dawning on her.

"This is what you were talking about last night, isn't it? When you said something about payback and all. You want me to spend my time off going to Tijuana on the mission trip with the kids."

Laurel's waving hand was artful and Carrie could tell she was trying not to smile. "Would you? It's only one week. You don't have to, of course. It would help

33

everybody out, though. You wouldn't have to sit bored to tears in your lonely apartment. And my poor children could spent their spring break helping build an orphanage like they'd planned, instead of having their mother hold them back."

Carrie tried not to laugh. "You realize, of course, that I still remember that you had the lead in the high school play three years in a row, don't you? I can still spot your acting skills a mile off, Laurel."

"It's not much of an act," Laurel said. "I really can't go to Tijuana right now, especially not to take care of twenty high school kids. And I know Rafe really needs the help."

"I'm sure he does. Anybody crazy enough to volunteer to take over high school youth activities at a church the size of Friedens Chapel needs all the help he can get." Carrie licked her lips for traces of whipped cream. "I haven't met him yet. How is this newcomer as a youth director, anyway?"

"The kids love him. I think he's pretty cool, too. He definitely gets a response out of them. I don't think anybody else could have convinced Ashleigh to go without running water for a week that easily."

"Hmm. Is there some way I can find out

more about the trip without totally committing myself?"

"Sure. There's another meeting at the church tomorrow night. That's one reason I tried to get you to come in this morning."

This was definitely the Laurel she knew and loved. "So you could soften me up in time to be a willing victim?"

"No, just to be a loving, concerned sister and aunt." Laurel came out from around the counter, and hugged Carrie without knocking into her cast. "We really will all appreciate this. And it will be fun. It's a definite win-win situation for everybody involved."

Carrie wasn't sure everything was quite that positive. But she wasn't about to argue with her sister. Especially not in Laurel's delicate condition. So Carrie nodded, tried what she hoped was a sweet smile and finished her mocha.

The meeting at church the next evening was more crowded than Carrie expected. The new youth minister must really be something if he could get this many teenagers and their parents together just to discuss a service project. The room fairly buzzed with excited kids talking to each other and their families.

It looked as if she would have plenty of

family company if she went on this trip. Not only were Jeremy and Ashleigh going, but, also, their cousin Trent was a couple rows up with his dad, her sister Claire's husband. The three teens were some of her favorite people. As the youngest sister in her family by a wide margin, she sometimes felt she had more in common with her sisters' teenage children than she did with her older, married sisters.

Pastor Ron called everybody in the crowded room to order, and opened with a prayer. Carrie was glad to see the older man here. He'd been the senior pastor of her church for most of her adult lifetime. If he was supporting this project, it had to be good.

He started talking about how important this mission project would be, not just for the high school youth, but for the whole congregation. From what Laurel had said, Carrie hadn't realized just how poor the people in Tijuana seemed to be.

"Mother Teresa called Tijuana, Mexico, one of the deepest pockets of poverty she had seen when she visited it in the late eighties," the pastor said, looking more solemn than usual. "For someone who had seen the worst slums of India to say that, you can imagine the conditions these people face every day of their lives. Very little has changed between then and now for many people in Tijuana.

"Jesus calls us to feed, clothe, house and otherwise help our brothers and sisters as if they were him. For all of us, as Christians, other people *are* Jesus when we do things in his name. How better to show our children what it is to serve Christ than to join them in this kind of mission work?"

Carrie felt tears welling up in her eyes. She hadn't thought about this in quite those terms. It was easier to commit to a project when it felt like a call to help people. Most of her reservations about going on the mission trip evaporated as Pastor Ron spoke.

"I wish that I could go with the crew. However, leaving for an entire week, beginning on Palm Sunday, would put too much of a burden on the other staff of Friedens Chapel. I'll just have to let all the pictures and stories that you kids and Rafe bring back, along with the chaperons who are going, tell the story to me."

Pastor Ron launched into a summary of how much money the youth group had raised so far to fund the project. The figures sounded impressive to Carrie. She understood now why one of the kids was always hitting her up to buy something their youth group was selling. All the money went to this project.

"So, is this cool, or what?" Ashleigh whispered to her. "I am *so* happy my dad is letting me do this. Once Laurel had to stay home, I didn't think he was going to say yes until you said you'd go."

"I said I'd think about it, Ash," Carrie whispered back.

Ashleigh's smooth brow rumpled. "You have to say yes, Carrie. Otherwise I won't get to go. Jeremy might not even get to go. Besides, I've been watching you. You're ready to sign up, aren't you?"

Carrie had to admit Ashleigh was right. Pastor Ron's inspiring speech had her mentally making a list of what to pack for a week in Mexico. This looked to be something that would definitely take her mind off being laid up and away from work. Surely even a one-handed rescue worker could make a difference in this project.

At the front of the room, the pastor stopped talking. "I've gone on long enough tonight. It's time to turn things over to the man that really knows what's going on, and can fill you parents and sponsors in. So let's give Dr. Rafe O'Connor his say." Pastor Ron waved to the side of the room while a cold chill went through Carrie.

Rafe, the kids' new youth leader, was none other than Dr. O'Connor? She'd heard Laurel and others mention several times that the youth leader was a doctor, but somehow she'd thought he was a Ph.D. from a Bible college or the like. She'd pictured a kindly soul closer to Pastor Ron's and her father's age. Someone scholarly with silver temples and a calm disposition.

But no, that wasn't the case. The man walking to the front of the room was definitely the same handsome, cocky young man she'd tangled with in the emergency room. And she'd just committed herself to spending one long week with him along with twenty teenagers for company.

The knowledge made her want to bolt, but the kids' enthusiasm for Rafe kept her in her seat. He was holding up his hands and trying to quiet the rowdy crowd so that he could speak. Hadn't he said something the other night about getting along well with teenagers? The kids' reaction seemed to prove that statement.

"I want to thank everybody for coming tonight. I know planning for this trip has meant a great deal of sacrifice for some of you parents and kids alike. And I know you're all giving of both your time and your money."

He looked so serious up there. Wasn't he going to say anything about having fun on the trip? The kids were using their whole spring break to do this.

"Casa Esperanza, the children's home we're going to, is very close to my heart. I can't begin to tell you how much it will mean to them to have us there for a week to build a new dormitory. And I can't begin to tell you what it will mean to your kids to do this work. I pray it will change everybody's hearts the way it has changed mine over the years."

Rafe O'Connor was serious and to the point. Still, something about him stirred Carrie and made her glad that she was going on this mission. Which probably meant that another doctor should examine her head. Still, for the first time since coming in contact with the high school gym floor, she felt her spirits lift. Maybe there was a reason why she broke her wrist. It certainly wasn't the April Fools' joke she'd thought it was.

Chapter Three

Carrie sought out her brother-in-law Ben Jericho in the crowd when the meeting was over and everyone was sipping punch and talking in small groups. It was easy to find Ben. He was always the guy surrounded by teenagers, looking almost as young and fit as they were, with his dark hair and coach's physique.

Tonight was no different. Ben looked great, and he was in the middle of a bunch of kids. He smiled when Carrie came up beside him, and waved off the next youth group member telling him a story so that she could speak.

"Tell me you're going along with this bunch," she said. "I want to count on at least one friendly adult face."

Having Ben along would be wonderful. If he were going, she might be able to get through the week without getting anywhere near Rafe O'Connor. But the words were barely out of her mouth when Ben

41

shook his head.

"Sorry. I just came so I could give Rafe the check for the last of Trent's deposit. And I promised Claire I'd make sure everything was still okay." He slung an arm around Trent's shoulder, and Carrie noticed that Trent had grown slightly taller than his dad. "She has problems with sending this strapping young man to what she thinks of as a dangerous area."

"Is it *that* dangerous?" Carrie felt a twinge of guilt at how quickly she was looking for a way out of this mission trip. Danger sounded like a good excuse to back out. And it was better than admitting the youth leader was possibly hazardous to her sanity.

But Ben wasn't helping her this time. "It could be. But Rafe has a lot of experience and we've lined up a massive amount of mission support for the project, both from America in the San Diego area just across the border, and from Mexico around Casa Esperanza. Enough support to satisfy me and pacify my wife."

Carrie watched her excuse evaporate. Of course she knew there weren't going to be any excuses good enough for her niece and nephews if she backed out. Not even breaking her other arm would work. No, she was too deep in to renege on her promise now. She was going to Tijuana with Rafe O'Connor.

"I hear you got your lucky break just in time to sub for Laurel." Ben motioned toward her cast, grinning as he spoke.

"Some lucky break. This cast itches already. And I still can't believe I'm going to be away from work until June."

Ben shrugged. "It could be worse. You've got a nice, clean break that is only going to keep you off work for a little while, not ruin your life. You're no worse off than any of the teenagers being coerced to go on this trip by their families because it will do them good."

"Great. I can be the den mother for unhappy campers. Maybe we can all sit together on the airplane and sing grumpy campfire songs while they autograph my cast." Ben started laughing, but Carrie didn't understand why.

"Airplane? Which part of the presentation did you miss, Carrie?" Ben's eyes sparkled like someone had just told him the best joke he'd heard all night.

"None of it, I thought. I heard the part about going coach."

"Not going coach, going *on* a coach. We couldn't afford to fly this whole crew to

43

Tijuana. With our budget we couldn't afford to fly this crew to Springfield, Missouri. You should feel lucky we can go with the church bus on loan from one of the bigger congregations in St. Louis. This one has air-conditioning, rest-room facilities, the whole bit."

Carrie's jaw dropped. "You mean they were talking about a coach, as in bus transportation? How long does it take to get to Mexico from here on a bus?" She tried to keep the rising note of panic out of her voice. The kids were counting on her. Now wasn't the time to show them how worried she was about this latest development.

"A couple of days. Two or three each way. There will be several drivers who can even help you two chaperon, so you can travel almost around the clock."

Carrie felt a little more relieved. "Great. When you say drivers, you do mean professionals, don't you? I don't have to take a hand in the driving, do I?"

"No, you're safe there. The cast probably lets you off anyway, even if you wanted to drive. They use a team of two or three that come with the coach as drivers. Rafe might drive just to spell somebody, but from what I hear, he actually likes to drive those things. There will be some breaks for the kids' sake to get out and stretch and eat at places along the way. It should be fun."

Carrie tried not to laugh. "Easy for you to say. You'll be back here running your sporting goods store, not trapped on a bus for two thousand miles with this bunch."

Ben's smile was all the answer she needed. Carrie excused herself to look for the soft drinks. She needed something to cool her off before she blew a gasket.

"So, what are we going to do with you?" Rafe O'Connor asked Jeremy Harrison and Ashleigh Jordan. Both of them stood in front of him nibbling on cookies while they discussed the trip. The two were among his favorite kids in this youth group. They had impressed him with their flexibility and enthusiasm. Once he'd found out that they'd been thrust into a situation of being instant siblings only months before, he was even more impressed with them. Their respective parents obviously loved them a great deal and worked quite hard to make their family situation work.

Rafe had to admire them for their hard work. There had been plenty of challenges in his own home growing up, but his parents had always been there for him and his brother and sister. It was good to see there were still families around like his.

Rafe had a little problem, though, and wondered how he could solve it and keep true to his strict rules. "Your mom was supposed to be my second-in-command," he told Jeremy. The lanky kid topped him by a good three inches, but he didn't use that advantage against Rafe. "Yesterday she calls and tells me that she can't go on the trip with us. That really puts me in a bind."

"Not for long." Jeremy's smile was bright. "My aunt's going to take her place. She's going to be off work for, like, a month or something and she told Mom she'd take over for her."

"You'll like Carrie. She's cool," Ashleigh chimed in. "She said I'm already her favorite niece."

Jeremy rolled his eyes. "Do the math, Ash. You're her *only* niece. And it's going to stay that way, because we are definitely having a brother in August."

Their banter made Rafe's thoughts spin in several directions at once. Laurel hadn't told him why she couldn't go on the trip, only citing health reasons she'd kept to herself. Listening to her kids, he knew her reason was the best one possible. And he agreed with Laurel one hundred percent. If she was expecting, the last thing he needed was to monitor her on a building site in Tijuana. There just weren't the medical facilities there for the kind of treatment she'd need in any emergency.

Meanwhile, Rafe wanted to talk about this aunt. He had a funny feeling that he knew who she was. And if he was right, he was going to be confronted with one unhappy woman in the very near future. "So, is your aunt here?" he asked, scanning the room and hoping he was wrong. Maybe there was another Carrie out of work for a while. Or maybe she just wasn't there and he could delay the storm. Either way would work.

"Yeah, she was over there talking to Trent's dad a minute ago." Ashleigh stood on her tiptoes, trying to see over the crowd in the room. "Oh, there she is. Getting a drink. I better go help her before she knocks over the cup. Doing things one-handed has to be hard."

Rafe could see a blaze of auburn hair over by the refreshment table, and according to Ashleigh, this Carrie was pouring her soda with one hand. This was going to be one very long mission trip.

In a moment Ashleigh was back with a

beautiful and familiar young woman in tow, complete with a casted right hand. Rafe tried not to roll his eyes. "Aunt Carrie, this is Rafe O'Connor, our youth minister. Rafe, this is my aunt Carrie. Or Jeremy's aunt, really, but he shares," Ashleigh said, making polite introductions.

"We've met, Ash." At least Carrie's expression wasn't as sour as Rafe feared it could have been. Rafe had a chance to take a good look at her. Either the lighting in here was kinder than it had been at the hospital, or Carrie had gotten more rest. She looked much better than he remembered.

Her blue eyes were clear, and the freckles on her cheeks didn't stand out in bold relief as they had when her arm was being set. "Dr. O'Connor is the guy who made sure I'd be wearing this cast for a couple months."

She arched one well-shaped eyebrow and tilted her head in his direction. "That wasn't on purpose, was it? You weren't already trolling for another mission partner?"

Rafe tried not to choke on his drink. He couldn't believe anybody would suggest such a thing. "Certainly not. I didn't even know who you were two days ago."

"And judging from the tone of your voice, if you had known, you wouldn't have picked me for this excursion anyway." Her chin stuck out in a manner that made her look like she wanted to take on the world. Rafe had no doubt that she did, frequently. Being on the receiving end of that look made him uneasy.

"I have to protest, Ms. Collins."

"Oh, call me Carrie and have done with it. We're going to be trapped on a bus together for days. And according to Ben, when we're not on the bus, we'll be out in the wild for most of the week. So you might as well be as friendly as possible, Dr. O'Connor."

"It's *Rafe,* please. Even the kids don't call me 'Dr. O'Connor' and I'd rather you didn't, either."

"Fine. So what were you protesting, Rafe? That you wouldn't have picked me on purpose to go on this trip?" Her eyes sparkled. She obviously enjoyed a good argument. Something about her combative manner made Rafe want to smile. She was pugnacious, but looked like she could be fun. Something about her intrigued him, and he wanted to aggravate her just to see her grin.

"Definitely. I can't say I wouldn't want

you along, Carrie. For all I know, you may be just the person the Lord wants me to take on this trip."

That didn't seem to be the answer she expected. Carrie actually looked taken aback. "Okay. Cool. I'm looking forward to it, in an odd sort of way."

That made him want to smile again. "How are you with a hammer and paint-brush?"

"Okay, I guess. Obviously I'd be better with two hands. But my dad made sure his girls all knew how to do the basics."

"Yeah, you should see her change a tire. When she has two hands free," Jeremy amended.

Carrie used her uncasted hand to ruffle his hair. She had to stand on tiptoe to reach her nephew's head. That endeared her to Rafe as nothing else had. "You're too kind." Rafe found himself wondering what her hand would feel like in his hair. Her touch with Jeremy was loving and playful.

"Okay, so you can change a tire. I'll call on you if we have bus problems." Why was he so touchy around Carrie? She was friendly enough and she seemed to mean well. So why did she aggravate him just by standing there? She made him feel like a short-tempered porcupine.

"I thought a mission group would take anybody who wasn't on their last legs." Vaguely upset, Carrie's cheeks flushed a pale pink, putting her freckles in relief. It was hard for Rafe to keep himself from running a fingertip against the velvet of her cheek. "What was Laurel bringing to this enterprise that I can't?"

Her question snapped Rafe back into the present quickly. He heard true hurt and concern in her voice and he hadn't meant to make her upset. He'd forgotten that women could compete with their siblings as fiercely as men. Time to think fast and say the right thing.

"Nothing. Except maybe a small knowledge of Spanish. Even your sister admitted that what she knew basically came from the radio and restaurant menus."

Carrie looked positively smug. "Three years in high school, and two in junior college while I was getting my licenses. Though I'll admit I'd have to brush up to say anything of much use, especially outside an ambulance."

"Really? I'm impressed. Maybe even with one hand you'll do okay. Can you help me keep these kids in line?"

She shook her head, sending auburn

waves bouncing. Her laugh was delightful. Rafe wanted to hear it again. "There, I have to admit I'm useless. I'm not the right person to keep them in line. I can entertain for you. But in my experience I haven't found too many kids in need of discipline."

"Then you've been lucky and hanging around the right kids. Remind me not to put you at the back of the bus."

Carrie's answering grin gave him goose-flesh. There were so many things about this spirited young woman that almost scared him. "You mean with the other troublemakers? That's where I fit in best."

Rafe wasn't sure what made him stick out his hand, first the right one, then when he realized that wouldn't work well, his left for a backward handshake. "I'm happy to have you along, Carrie. Welcome to the team."

She took his hand. Her grip was surprisingly warm and firm. He felt as if he was being challenged to a contest. If this had been one of the youth group kids he'd say he was being tested. He gripped her hand back firmly, enjoying the contact of their skin.

Rafe had to admit that for most of his life, women did not challenge him. As a doctor he was used to being listened to and obeyed. As youth group leader, he was as much in charge as he was in the emergency room. Having Carrie take him on might be an entertaining challenge, after all. It was with a feeling of regret that Rafe let her hand go and watched her leave.

Carrie was glad the drive back to Laurel and Jesse's wasn't too long. She was tired tonight, and her arm ached inside the cast. She was looking forward to resting at home. Meanwhile, she had to drive Jeremy and Ashleigh home.

"So isn't he awesome? Rafe, I mean. I think it's so cool you already know him," Ashleigh bubbled. Carrie searched for a way to answer her kindly and still be honest.

"We didn't meet under the best circumstances. So I don't think he's as awesome as you guys do. I can see why there are so many kids coming to youth group." Carrie had to admit Rafe O'Connor had a strong, magnetic personality. She wasn't sure why his strength seemed to push her away as much as it drew the kids toward him.

"You don't like him much, do you?" Jeremy's voice was soft. "It's not just a grudge, is it? Because of the cast."

"Could be," Carrie admitted. "I'm not

real happy to be off work for this long, and he is the guy responsible."

"Oh, yeah?" Jeremy sounded skeptical.

She tried to explain how she felt. "It could have gone either way. I know people who have had this same fracture and just wore a splint."

"Doing what kind of job? Heavy active stuff like you do?"

"Well, no, not really."

"Thought not. And what about your history? Mom says you and I are about tied for the number of broken bones."

"She's probably right. At least mine have come mostly in the line of duty."

"Right. Like this one, huh?" For once Carrie wasn't so thrilled her nephew was an intelligent young man. He seemed destined for a career in law, judging from his argument skills.

"Hey, for the most part they have. And I guess I have to admit that even Rafe said that some people do wear splints. In this case neither he nor the orthopedic specialist were real enthusiastic about me wearing one."

"Because it was a bad break?"

"That, too." She couldn't lie to Jeremy, as much as she wanted to. Telling the truth got her in trouble sometimes, but she wasn't about to stop now. "But mostly because I was honest with them and admitted I wouldn't keep the splint on like I was supposed to."

Jeremy's answer was a crow of pure delight. "I knew it! So what does Rafe have to do with that? He isn't the one who made you play volleyball, is he?"

"Point taken." Carrie answered through clenched teeth. "He is very aggravating, though."

Ashleigh sniffed. "I still think he's awesome."

"Aw, you just say that because you think he's cute. All the girls think he's cute. Don't think we haven't heard you giggling. . . ."

Carrie had to work fast to keep the fight between her niece and nephew from escalating. "That's enough, Jeremy. Remember, I can tell Ashleigh stories you'd probably rather not have her hear. So if you tease her, I'll make sure she has plenty of ammunition to tease back."

"Oh, man. You'd do it, too."

"In a heartbeat. Now, is there something you'd like to tell your sister?"

There was silence from Jeremy's side of the back seat. "I guess. Sorry about what I said. I know that his looks aren't the only reason you think Rafe is awesome."

"Good. You know I have more depth than that." Ashleigh sounded more mature than Carrie expected. Then she sighed. "But that means I don't get to hear any of Carrie's stories."

"Not yet. I can't imagine Jeremy will be good for so long that you'll never hear them, Ashleigh."

"Great. I need ammunition. I'm not used to having a big brother yet. They can be pretty ratty people sometimes."

"Sounds like big sisters. I think that's the older sibling's job." Carrie concentrated on the road for a few minutes. She wondered how she could thank her big sister for getting her involved in this mission trip. Of all the "pretty ratty" things Laurel had done to her since they were kids growing up, this one took the cake.

Chapter Four

"Okay, let's see that packing list again," Carrie said to Ashleigh, holding out her hand. "I know that everything is supposed to fit in one duffel bag. And I don't understand how."

Carrie had used the last two weeks to get comfortable with the idea of being with Rafe and the kids for eight days. Truth be known, it had taken most of that time to get used to the idea of Rafe being her constant companion for that long than anything else. So far, with all the planning and work that needed to be done, she had managed not to be alone with him.

When she wasn't going to team meetings, her time was taken up planning for the trip. She'd shopped for the clothing and supplies she'd need. Now there were two days before they left and she was as ready as she would ever be. Today was packing day. They'd devoted the afternoon to Ashleigh's stuff, and tonight Carrie would pack her own duffel bag.

There were clothing and accessories strewn all over the floor. Carrie couldn't complain much because she expected her things were going to look much the same when she packed.

"It would be easy if you didn't need so much weird stuff," Jeremy called from his room, sounding terribly smug and male.

Ashleigh tossed her head, indicating her exasperation with Jeremy. "What do you mean, weird stuff?"

"Four kinds of shampoo and cutesy little socks and those things you hold your hair back with. How about just jeans, T-shirts and shorts? If you just packed the basic stuff, plus toothpaste and soap, it would all fit in the duffel. Mine does. Hey, look, I've even got room for one of my gallons of water."

Jeremy was risking life and limb with that last statement, especially since he stuck his head into Ashleigh's doorway while he said it. She looked like she wanted to toss a tennis shoe at him.

"And we're very proud of you, I'm sure." Carrie tried not to sound too sarcastic. Jeremy went back down the hall to his own room, cackling.

Carrie stifled a laugh. "Ash, let's unpack

everything again and figure out what can stay here."

"Sounds like a logical plan," Laurel said as she came into the room. She had always been the voice of reason. At times Carrie resented having two cool, calm and quite feminine older sisters to compete with. But then there were times like this when she valued their advice.

"How are you feeling?" Carrie asked her sister.

"Fine. I didn't need a nap today and I managed to eat breakfast this morning. It was only dry graham crackers, but it's a move in the right direction."

"If you say so. Congratulations." But Carrie wasn't sure whether keeping down dry crackers and not napping was worth celebrating. Her sisters set great store by their kids, and even she had to admit that once they got older they were a lot of fun. They'd been fun when they were toddlers and she'd been a teenager, but she hadn't really known what to do with them.

Maybe when she found the kind of love that her sisters had, she'd consider marriage and children. So far, nothing had come along. When she was younger she'd wondered why there didn't seem to be a man in God's plans for her. At twenty-eight, Carrie was beginning to think that maybe she was one of those people who were better off single.

Like Rafe O'Connor. He seemed perfectly happy being single, and he certainly couldn't do everything he wanted to do saddled with a wife and kids, could he? Carrie knew what working at Fire and Rescue did to marriages. She could just imagine what emergency medicine, which usually meant anywhere from twelve to twenty-four hours on duty at a time, would do for a relationship.

And on top of his grueling work schedule, Rafe managed to volunteer at the church youth group, and who knew what else. For that she had to admire him. At least he knew his limitations and hadn't chosen to make some poor woman miserable. Although, as she sat folding one of Ashleigh's T-shirts so it would go in a duffel, Carrie mused whether most women would be that miserable married to Rafe O'Connor.

"Okay, I don't know where your brain has gone off to, but that one's done," Laurel said, gently taking the T-shirt out of Carrie's hands and putting it in Ashleigh's duffel. Carrie felt the back of her neck flush redder than her hair. How did her thoughts get wrapped around one stubborn, handsome man so quickly? She shook herself out of her reverie and went back to folding shirts.

As predicted, at nine in the evening Carrie's bedroom looked like Ashleigh's had earlier. It was frustrating to be surrounded by so many piles of clothing and supplies and know that she was nowhere near getting it to fit in one bag. How had Jeremy got all his stuff *and* a gallon of water in the same size bag?

She needed a break. She needed a cookie, in fact. Not that there were any in the apartment. Knowing she'd be gone for over a week, she'd let the grocery supply get even slimmer than usual, which meant that her normally bare pantry was incredibly empty. The refrigerator held one container of yogurt, a carton with enough milk for tomorrow's bowl of cereal and a few odd jars of ketchup, mustard and pickles.

There wasn't much she could make a snack out of. So there was no incentive to pack the rest of her stuff by promising she could have a cookie break in fifteen minutes. She could only have an ice-water break. How thrilling.

Laurel had finally shown them a trick for

folding T-shirts this afternoon that made Ashleigh's luggage manageable. Carrie looked down at her pile of shirts, trying to remember how to work her sister's magic. With one good arm and clumsy fingers poking out of her cast, she wasn't able to roll the shirts in the same neat cylinders Laurel had managed. But they looked okay, and putting them in the bag that way did save more room for other things.

Straightening her back, Carrie stretched and finally got off the bedroom floor to stand and work the kinks out of her neck and back. Midway through a delicious stretch that made her neck pop, the doorbell rang. She tried to figure out who on earth would be at her front door at nine o'clock on a Thursday night.

When she looked out the peephole, Carrie couldn't believe what she was seeing. Rafe O'Connor, in jeans and a pale sport shirt, stood in the hallway of her apartment building. She didn't realize he had her address, much less knew where she lived. Of course her address was on many forms at church, but she'd never considered he'd take the time to look it up.

"Just a minute," she called out, frantically raking her good hand through her hair. There was nothing she could do about her rumpled clothes or the fact that she wore no makeup.

She was going to make a lovely impression on this man. He'd think she was the most casual person in the world. True, she didn't always dress up, but Rafe had managed to catch her at her worst every time but the meeting at church, when she'd been trying to dress neatly. Why did it seem like everything she owned had sleeves that wouldn't fit over her cast?

She fumbled with the locks, and finally opened the door. "Hi. You surprised me. Want to come in?"

"I guess I did surprise you." Carrie wasn't sure quite what Rafe meant by that. He was smiling, and seemed to be regarding her attire in a way that made her wish more than ever for a closetful of designer sportswear. "You sure you don't mind me coming in?"

"Not at all. Please." She motioned with her good hand, and Rafe entered her apartment. "I'd offer you something to eat or drink, but there's not much here. I'm trying to get the refrigerator empty before we leave."

"I know what you mean. If this were my place, our choices would be one ancient can of soda or ice water. I'm even out of coffee."

"So am I. But when you say that it sounds like it's a tragedy."

"It is. I'm going to be loads of fun without any coffee for a week. But then I won't have the pressures of the emergency room to deal with, so maybe things will be better."

Carrie studied Rafe in her living room. He looked comfortable without his white coat. Obviously cowboy boots and worn jeans were his normal attire. Maybe he didn't care about her clothes after all.

"Won't the folks at Casa Esperanza make sure you're taken care of? I mean, if we're building a wing for them, surely they'll treat everyone well."

"They will. Just as well as they can and know how. But I tell them to concentrate on the youth group kids when we go down there, not the adults. I've been doing this stuff with Casa Esperanza for years wherever I've worked and lived. And they concentrate on the kids, which is just the way I want it."

"Good. I won't have to worry much, because I still eat like a kid — sugared cereal for breakfast, cola for my caffeine buzz, unless Laurel makes me a mocha."

"And that's not real coffee. It's pretend coffee with whipped cream and chocolate."

Was there a ghost of a smile on Rafe's lips? "So, you want to go get one?"

"Sure. We can't go to Laurel's, though. She shut The Right Place down early tonight so that everybody would go home and finish packing."

"There has to be someplace else to get coffee here, doesn't there?"

"How do you feel about root beer? I know Chuck's out on the highway is open until midnight, and I think there's a float that's calling my name."

This time she definitely saw a smile. It looked good on Rafe, and Carrie wondered what she would have to do to make it a permanent expression. "You give me the directions, I'll get there. Does Chuck make chili to go with those floats?"

"The best. Give me five minutes and we'll be out the door," Carrie called over her shoulder as she headed to the bedroom. Surely somewhere among the packing mess she could find shoes she could slip on without help, and a clean shirt that didn't button.

"Was this just a social call because we both have empty pantries?" Carrie sipped some more of her float through the straw.

"Not totally. It dawned on me during my

65

shift today that we'd never been alone together." Rafe eyed his chili dog suspiciously. "This thing isn't going to be near spicy enough, is it? I should have asked for more jalapeños."

"I should have known that Missouri chili wasn't going to be spicy enough for you. And why is it so important that we be alone together?"

Rafe didn't seem to focus on her question. "What do you mean, your chili wouldn't be hot enough for me? Because of my Mexican roots?" He seemed to be challenging her.

"Mexico? I figured you were from Texas. The boots, the jeans. Somehow your whole demeanor says 'cowboy' to me."

He relaxed in his seat. "Oh. Okay. There's a little Texas in there. A little more California, and a lot of Mexico. Does that change your opinion of me?"

"Should it? I can't see why it would."

"Have you ever been out West? I forget that brown people just aren't common enough to be looked down on as much here."

"Brown people? What do you mean?" People were people. Carrie didn't tend to classify them by skin tone.

"Latinos. Chicanos. People of Mexican

or Central American heritage. And those are only the polite names."

"Does it really make a difference?"

Rafe shook his head. "You never cease to surprise me, Carrie. You're so naive."

"I didn't come out here with you to be insulted." Carrie's cheeks started to burn. "And I don't think I'm that naive. I see a lot in my job, as much as you do probably."

"You see as much as Friedens, Missouri, will let you see." Rafe held up his hand, stopping her protest before she opened her mouth. "I didn't mean to insult you. It's just that there's a big world out there that you can't see from this little corner. And most of it isn't very kind or forgiving. Especially if you aren't light-skinned, middle-class and all-American. Preferably with several ancestors you can trace back to the right parts of Europe."

"I think you're wrong about that."

"Okay. You're entitled to your opinion. However I'll check in with you after two days in Tijuana and see if it still holds true. I want you to see Casa Esperanza and the kids who live there. See them like I have, and then tell me that I'm wrong."

"That's fine. I think I will." Carrie looked across the table at Rafe. His eyes

67

glowed with emotion and she could not resist the desire to reach out to him. "Can we talk about something else? Almost anything else?" She only had one hand she could use to grasp his hand with.

Surprisingly, he didn't pull back, nor did he argue. "Yes, we can. This wasn't at all the way I expected our conversation to go. I really only wanted to get to know you better. How do you do that?"

She was conscious of the strong, warm grip of his fingers. It wasn't too hard or demanding. Just firm enough, making her want to stay here, linked to him, not letting go. "Do what?"

"Get me all confused. Start me on tracks I never intended to travel. Stir me up. Around you I feel like a different person, Carrie."

She could feel her cheeks flushing. "Is that good or bad?"

His answering laugh was husky, and he kept hold of her hand. "Both, I think. I'm not used to being challenged the way you challenge me. Maybe my opinions aren't always on target for everything. Maybe I need that challenge."

Carrie found herself grinning back. "Now I can turn your words back at you. See if you still feel you need the challenge after we've been together awhile. After about two days in Tijuana?"

"Sounds fair." He let go of her fingers. "How about you finish that float and I take you home? We've got plenty to do, and very little time to accomplish it before we leave on our trip."

Carrie felt like groaning. That sounded so serious, so Rafe. "I guess so. If I can't talk you into another float for the road."

"Never. I don't drink and drive, especially when it's root beer. Stains the upholstery."

That comment made Carrie want to lean over and kiss Rafe, just for the shock value. Before she could change her mind, she did it. It wasn't the longest kiss Carrie had ever given anyone, but it definitely packed more punch than anything she'd ever experienced. Just touching Rafe's soft, warm lips with hers made her skin tingle as if charged with electricity. In an instant she realized that the "shock value" of the kiss was as much her reaction as it was in what she expected out of him.

The biggest surprise was that Rafe kissed her back as if he'd been thinking the same thing she had. When he pulled away after a few seconds, he smiled wider than she'd ever seen him smile. "That was nice. Very,

very nice. But I hope that you got that out of your system," he told her. "Because no matter how much fun it was, we can't do that in front of the kids. Thanks for getting it out of the way here."

Carrie's head was spinning. "You're welcome, I think. We couldn't do that in front of the kids. We have to set a good example." She was aware she was babbling, and closed her mouth before she said anything more.

Rafe nodded his head. He seemed to be stirred up by their kiss, for all his talk of getting it out of the way. Had this meant something to both of them? Carrie wasn't sure. She tried to figure out this complicated man. Maybe Rafe wasn't all business. And maybe, just maybe, this trip would turn out to be a very good thing after all.

Chapter Five

"Are you sure that's all the room we have for the luggage?" Ben Jericho leaned back out of the bottom compartment of the bus. The sun was just dawning on Palm Sunday and all Carrie could see of her brother-in-law was surrounded by piles of duffel bags.

"That's it, pardner." The bus driver was a grizzled old soul who looked as if he should be driving a chuck wagon on a cattle drive. He'd introduced himself as Jake. "Just Jake, ma'am, and this here's Letty." Letty, his wife, looked as if she'd be more at home sitting in a rocker, knitting sweaters, but Jake assured them all that she could handle the bus and the teenagers as well as he could. "Better, if we're in heavy traffic. She has the patience for it and I'm afraid I don't."

Carrie had the idea that Jake and Letty were the same age as her father and his wife, Gloria, which would put them right around sixty years old. They definitely had more silver hair than Hank and Gloria, and looked like they spent a good deal more time outdoors.

"Now I see why you had us all pack so tightly," she told Rafe, who was standing a few feet behind Ben surveying the sea of luggage. "We'll be lucky to get this all stowed, along with the water."

"I could still make most of the girls ditch at least half a bag, I'm sure." Rafe surveyed the piles of belongings. "Even though I stressed that we can't bring anything electric, and there's no sense in bringing any nice clothes, wanna bet we've got a fair amount of both?"

"Aw, we're not all that dumb," Carrie argued. At the same time she had to admit to having one khaki jumper in her duffel that probably didn't fit in the "work clothes" category. But she agreed with Ashleigh that it felt wrong somehow to be bringing nothing but jeans, shorts and T-shirts for a week.

"Okay, everybody listen up," Rafe called, motioning toward his excited teen charges. "We're short of space here and long on stuff. I want everybody to reclaim his or her own luggage and try to remove one item. If it's not your Bible, your toothbrush, or work clothes and it's in your bag, it's fair game for consideration. Whatever you pull, show it to me first and then leave it with your parents."

All the kids groaned. So did most of the parents. Jake smiled. "It won't make you popular with them, but that will go a-ways toward trimming down the luggage compartment. Thanks."

"Anytime. Do you want to say anything to the group before we get going?" Rafe asked.

"Not particularly," Jake answered. "They look like a fine bunch of kids. We should get along real well."

Carrie was glad to hear somebody shared her opinion of this bunch of teenagers. Rafe was so serious about everything that she wasn't sure that he gave the kids enough credit. Sure, most of them were horsing around this morning, but they were excited and nervous.

Many of them hadn't ever been away from their families for a week. Those that had had probably stayed with grandparents or other relatives, or maybe had gone to church camp.

This was going to be more of a challenge than church camp. Carrie looked for her duffel among the others and hauled it out. "I don't have a parent with me. Can I leave stuff with you?" she asked Ben.

"Sure. I'll make sure it gets back home to Claire, who will probably wash it and iron it for you."

"Great." Carrie undid the heavy zipper of her bag and rooted around as best she could one-handed. The fingers poking out of her cast still weren't much good for fine motor things like sorting through a suitcase. In a moment she found the jumper and pulled it out of the bottom of the stack. She had to admit the bag was far easier to zip without that item of clothing.

She handed it to Ben, who was taking a button-down shirt from Trent. "Your mom made you put that in there, didn't she?"

His son just looked at him. "You think I would bring a shirt with a collar on a trip like this?"

Ben grinned. "I'll tell her Rafe made you get rid of it."

"Fine. Get me in trouble," Rafe said behind them. Carrie whirled around quickly to catch the expression on his face. It was the first time she'd heard him this lighthearted. "Actually I don't mind. Anything you tell her to get that shirt out of his bag is cool. If you want to make me the bad guy, go ahead."

Rafe was smiling, and Carrie thought it

improved his good looks quite a bit. She'd seen him tease her, and others, but with a fleeting grin on his face. But this was an honest smile, and it made Rafe look lit from within.

"Are you that excited to get going?" Carrie asked.

He smiled even more broadly. "Well, sure. Aren't you?"

"Yeah, but I get excited by the least little thing. I didn't think you were capable of this much enthusiasm."

"Think again. As far as I'm concerned, this is the best week of the year. This is better than Christmas and I'm ready to go." Carrie could only watch in surprise, trying to keep her mouth from hanging open as Rafe O'Connor walked to the next gaggle of teens and adults. The man was actually whistling a happy tune.

Rafe sat on the coach and considered what he'd told Carrie. It wasn't quite the truth — right now he felt like a kid on Christmas Eve. Sitting in the second row of coach seats he wanted to squirm like a six-year-old. Four hours into the trip, they'd already made it to Joplin, Missouri. Jake had stopped driving and let his wife take a turn. In less than a hundred miles they'd be to Tulsa. Then they'd have a late lunch at the first of several churches along the way whose contingent would feed the kids and let them run around for a while to burn off some energy.

He didn't dare look behind him. Carrie was a few rows behind him, not in the very back of the bus, as he'd thought. She had at least six of the kids involved in singing some awful, repetitive camp song that involved snapping and clapping. Though it added to Rafe's impatience, it kept them from asking "Are we there yet?" so he was happy they were making the racket.

It was difficult to be thankful for Carrie. He knew there had to be some great purpose involved in God's crazy stirring up of his long-awaited and well-planned mission trip. It was just that Rafe had no idea what that reason was.

Maybe the impetuous ball of energy, otherwise known as Carrie, needed to learn something from him. Maybe there was something in Mexico that the Lord particularly wanted to show to her. That had to be the answer. Because there couldn't possibly be anything that he could learn from this woman by spending a week in her company.

That kiss had been nice. The thought

came to him unbidden, making him sit up even straighter in the seat he shared with only his clipboard and his planner. But that kiss had been just another example of Carrie's rash nature. She hadn't put any thought into the action at all, or given it the careful deliberation one should have before kissing someone you'd only known for a few short weeks. That's what he would have done. Which was probably why he'd enjoyed that unexpected kiss so much, if he could be truly honest with himself.

Though the kiss had been nice, it wasn't going to come back and haunt him on the bus. And it certainly wasn't the reason why Carrie was on this trip. He didn't need any romantic entanglements in his life right now, and surely God knew that as well as he did.

"Yo, Rafe, think fast!" A beach ball sailed over the back of the seat and landed on his clipboard. The laughter swelled around him quicker than he could react to the missile scattering his papers and sending his pencil rolling under the seat in front of him.

He sprang into the aisle before he could breathe. "All right, no more of that. And I want the guilty party up here, on the double."

"For a doctor you sure have lousy reflexes." Carrie grinned, unrepentant. He should have known that even with only one good arm, she'd thrown the ball. She stood up where she was, but he waved her away. There was no sense in getting her next to him.

"But you have lousy role-model skills if you really threw that ball," he fired back. "We're the grown-ups. Try to act like one, okay?"

Her reaction made him feel like he'd yelled at a puppy. The light went out of her eyes, and the kids around her went silent and serious. Rafe looked at all of them, regretting showing so much anger. He reined in the impulse to explode and took a deep breath instead.

"Sure. I guess it was a dumb move. I'm sorry." Ignoring his request for her to stay where she was, she moved up the aisle as quickly as her cast and the crowd of kids would allow.

"No more incoming objects without warning, and that goes for everybody, okay? I've got paperwork under four seats now." Rafe glared at the kids.

"I'm sorry. I didn't realize you were working up there. Can I help you pick everything up?" Carrie looked more contrite than he expected she would.

"Don't bother. I'll pick it up myself in a minute. If I can find my pencil. Hey, Trent," he called to the front of the bus. "See if you can find a bright red pencil under your seat, or Missy's."

"I'd like to help." Carrie followed him up the aisle.

"Suit yourself." He eased into his seat and started sorting papers. The beach ball had been put in the seat next to his, and it bobbed with the motion of the coach. He lowered his voice as Carrie moved the ball and sat down beside him. "Nice shot, by the way. But like I said, lousy role model."

"I know. But it did break up some tension back there. Everybody's getting squirmy and eager to walk around for a while. I should have thought before I aimed it at you, though." She gathered up the sheaf of papers that had gone onto the floor and the aisle. "I think these are back in order."

Rafe took the papers. "I hope so. Once we eat at the church in Tulsa, how about coming up with some games to play with that beach ball? Maybe relay races to burn off some steam, okay?"

"Will do. No problem." Carrie's smile was lopsided as she made her way back down the aisle of the moving coach. He almost felt like apologizing for chewing her out. They were going to be the adults together on this trip for a week. It was silly to start off badly. He would try to be civil in Tulsa. Maybe even more than civil, more like complimentary.

He rifled through the papers Carrie had handed back. Surprisingly they were in the right order, all of them. Turning the first sheet over to the blank side, he reached for his pencil to start making a list of some sort.

But there was no pencil. Apparently Trent hadn't found it yet. He peered under the seat, but was unable to see much under there. When he straightened up, Missy was in the seat beside him. "She likes you, you know."

The girl held out his pencil and he took it from her. She looked much younger than a high school freshman. She was small and impish, almost fragile looking. Her thin legs looked like they were more used to bandaged knees than high heels. And right now she seemed to be speaking a foreign language.

"What are you talking about?" Even after growing up with a sister, Rafe couldn't understand women. Not the young ones like Missy, or the slightly older ones like Carrie. He spoke Spanish and English, and even a tiny bit of Portuguese. But he did not speak their language.

"Carrie. The beach ball thing was sorta fifth grade. But I'm pretty sure she likes you."

"Fifth grade." He echoed the phrase, still trying to understand what Missy was saying.

"Remember when you were in fifth grade and the girls chased the boys and the boys chased the girls?" Missy looked like somebody who could still be in fifth grade herself. If she put her pale hair up in pigtails, the image would be complete. "My mom always told me the same thing when I complained. She said that they wouldn't bother chasing you if they didn't like you."

"So you think because Carrie beaned me with a beach ball, she likes me?"

"Sure. Not all adults know exactly what to do with things like that."

"I see. It couldn't just be a case of boredom or poor aim?" Both sounded more likely to him than Carrie Collins liking him.

"I guess it could be. Who else would she be trying to hit, though? And as far as boredom, we're all bored."

"I'm not." Rafe felt like he was back on high school debate team again. "I've got plenty to do and nobody will let me do it. That sounds like the opposite of boredom to me."

Missy shrugged slight shoulders. "Have it your way. I still say she likes you. You're always asking us what we're going to do about things like that. When you present us with a problem, that's the first thing you ask."

"You're right. I do say that a lot." Thrown back in his face, Rafe's own words sounded more like a challenge. "Even if you're right, though, Missy, there's only one thing I can do about this."

"Really?" Her young eyes showed more questioning and wisdom than he thought possible.

"Right. The same thing I tell you to do after I ask you what you're going to do. Put all your troubles in God's hands and go about doing what you know He wants you to do."

Missy sighed. "But that's so boring and mature. Wouldn't you have more fun if you got a water balloon and fired it back at Carrie? To tell her you liked her, too?"

"I'm a boring, mature kind of guy. This is more my speed." Rafe stopped there. He wasn't about to share with a fourteen-year-old the secret that he had no idea if he liked Carrie Collins, too. Or that the thought of searching his heart to find out terrified him. "Besides, water balloons and people in casts don't mix. Let that be your medical fact for the day."

"If you say so." Missy slipped back into her own seat, looking somewhat glum. Rafe went back to his lists and plans. With every bump of the coach wheels on the pavement, Missy's words echoed in his head. Carrie Collins liked him? Was that possible? Why did it even matter? And could he really leave such a weighty matter totally in God's hands?

Carrie sat in her seat and watched the scenery go by. Oklahoma was incredibly flat. She tried counting trees for a while, but there weren't all that many of them, and they all looked alike. After a while she was sure she'd counted the same tree forty-seven times.

How could she have been so stupid? Rafe already thought she was a brainless, immature fool. Now he was probably sure of it. She'd just been trying to lighten the atmosphere and give the kids, and the truth be told, her, some entertainment.

She didn't have any idea that he'd react to being bopped with a beach ball as if she'd declared World War III.

Now she sat back here feeling really dumb and immature. Why did this have to happen just when she'd begun to feel they were making some headway toward an adult relationship? Or at least a friendship based on respect.

Now she was glad she'd kissed him back in Friedens while she had the chance, before the trip. Because that would probably be the only time that was likely to happen. Carrie was surprised that gave her a pang of regret. For all his aggravating characteristics, there were a lot of things to like about Rafe. He was honest and intense and hardworking. He wasn't bad looking at all, and he got along well with teenagers.

Unfortunately the two of them were like oil and water. She couldn't quite understand why he brought out the child in her, when only a mature, rational adult was likely to impress him. Just her luck that he made her act lighthearted but preferred the serious type of woman she could never be.

Even when they pulled into the parking lot of the church in Tulsa, Carrie's mood hadn't lifted. She followed the kids off the bus, with more of them trailing behind her as they got out and stretched their arms and legs on the pavement.

It was only after she counted heads and made sure everybody was where they were supposed to be that Carrie took a good look at the pastor who had come to meet them outside the church. Carrie could hardly believe her eyes.

He was tall and lean, with the same outdoorsy look as Rafe, and it didn't surprise her to see that he was wearing cowboy boots. This was Oklahoma. His angular face mirrored Rafe's, but his hair was a dark, glossy red with hints of a brown so dark it was almost black. He was already talking in an animated fashion to Rafe as if they knew each other well.

Carrie looked around for the signboard of the church. Sure enough, under Faith Christian Fellowship Welcomes You there was a list of the pastors. The first assistant listed was Rob O'Connor.

"You didn't tell me this trip was planned as a family reunion," Carrie said, walking up to the two men. The closer she got to them, the more similarities she found.

"Didn't seem important. He's only my kid brother," Rafe shot back. "Carrie Collins, my youngest brother, Roberto. And

Rob, this is Carrie."

"Let me guess. You have an announcement to make," Rob said, clapping his brother on the back. "It's about time."

Carrie was so stunned by Rob's remark, it took her a minute to find her tongue. Rafe wasn't as hampered by shock, so he spoke quicker. She knew that both she and Rafe were saying the same things — "No. No announcement. No nothing." — in voices that were louder than Rob expected. Carrie had thought before that Rafe O'Connor was totally unflappable. Now she saw that all it took was a little brotherly love to make him turn a shade of red she never dreamed possible. Looking at Rafe, she wondered what color her own face was. Probably a lovely pink that matched his. Surrounded by roaring teenagers who had all heard Rob's question, she felt like her face was on fire.

Chapter Six

"Sorry about the misunderstanding, Carrie." Rob O'Connor and Carrie stood together in the line where women from the church were dishing out a meal for the teens. His church had a nice multipurpose room attached to a kitchen big enough to feed a busload of hungry kids.

"Whatever gave you that idea, anyway?" Since their quick denials Carrie had wondered what Rob had seen to make him think they were a couple.

Rob blushed the same shade Rafe had been earlier. "I don't know. He looked so happy. And I've got to tell you, there's never been such an attractive young woman on any of his mission trips before. I though something good was actually happening to my brother. He deserves a bit of happiness, but he never goes looking for it."

"Never?" Carrie found herself extremely interested in this information about Rafe.

"Not that I've seen. I know a career in medicine keeps you pretty busy. We all thought, though, that once his internship and residency were over and he had a regular job someplace, things might change. But true to form, Rafe picks a specialty like emergency medicine that leaves no time for a personal life."

"If I hadn't broken my arm we would have met eventually, anyway. I work Fire and Rescue for the county next to where his hospital is located."

"Which definitely makes you even more off-limits, according to my brother's strict code of ethics, than you would have been as just a patient. Patients eventually get better and become somebody else's problem. Honestly, I'm really sorry I made that mistake."

"Not as sorry as you would be if we were staying the night." Rafe came up behind his brother, and Carrie noticed the man actually jumped.

"Aw, you wouldn't do anything rude to a man of the cloth, would you?"

"Me? Never." Rafe didn't sound very convincing to Carrie. His voice was light and teasing and she liked it more than she cared to admit. "I would be happy, however, to tell your own youth group what your nickname was in junior high. Hey, I bet Sharon doesn't even know that yet." Rafe raised his head up above the others and looked into the kitchen where women were serving food at a long window.

Rob pushed gently on his brother's shoulders. "Sure she does. Trust me on that one."

"Sharon is . . . ?" Carrie asked, fairly sure she knew the answer.

"My wife. She's that sweet blond girl on the end who's handing out brownies. The one you're going to keep away from my fiendish brother, right?" Rob managed to say with a smile. He still had a hand on Rafe's shoulder, and seemed to be reminding his older brother that they were matched in size and weight. If Rafe felt at all threatened, it didn't show.

"Honest, I'll be good. Besides, we're only here for an hour or two. Peace, okay?" His free hand came around and clapped his brother on the shoulder, then they separated.

"Sure, man." Rob turned back to Carrie as the line moved forward. "So if you guys aren't an item, how did he ever talk you into going on one of these trips?"

"I've got a niece and nephew in the crew, and I'm filling in for their mom. She's sort of indisposed right now. And I was off work anyway, thanks to your brother." She lifted her cast.

"You didn't set that. It's not neat enough."

"Now I'm really going to have to go get Sharon," Rafe said. "There was a real orthopedist on duty so I didn't have to do much wrapping."

"Be happy he didn't have to do that cast. And be even happier that he didn't have to stitch you up," Rob said. "You'd still be there. He takes such picky little stitches."

"I haven't heard anybody else complain." This whole sparring match made Carrie want to giggle. At first she'd wondered if meeting some of Rafe's family was such a good thing. When Rob had mistaken them for a couple, she was sure it would add to the friction between them. Now, though, she was seeing a different side of Rafe, and she liked it.

"Ay, Rafael . . ." Rob began, and finished his sentence in Spanish so fast that Carrie had trouble following him.

Rafe fired back something equally fast, and Carrie felt left out. "Would you two like to share with the rest of the class? In English?"

"Not necessarily." Rafe's answer came so

quickly she was sure that whatever they were talking about had something to do with her. "Let's just say Rob has a higher opinion of you than I do. Of course, he hasn't been beaned in the head with a beach ball yet."

"If that's the worst she ever does to a hard case like you, count yourself lucky, brother. But then, if Renata never did you permanent harm, you must be living a charmed life."

"Who's Renata?" Carrie wondered if this was an old girlfriend she should be aware of, or another sibling she'd meet on the trip.

Rafe seemed happy to answer. "Our sister. Older than Rob, younger than me, and a terror when we were all growing up. Naturally it fell to me to provide the good example and keep her in line. Of course now she's a high school principal, so I have nothing but the utmost respect for her."

Rob smirked. "Right. You're just saying that because I'm listening and you know I'll tell her if you make any comments. You guys stopping through Albuquerque?"

"I figured on it. Renata said she could do brunch for this rowdy bunch tomorrow."

"All right," Rob crowed. "Sit next to me

at lunch, Carrie, and I'll tell you things to ask my sister that will forever change your view of this fine, upstanding gentleman."

Carrie knew she was grinning as broadly as Rob was. "I can hardly wait."

In the Texas darkness the quiet highway was almost mesmerizing. Rafe kept both hands on the big steering wheel of the coach, wishing he had louder, more upbeat music to drive to. But that would keep the kids awake.

In the long run, this was better. The quiet gospel tape Jake played over the speaker system before they switched drivers had lulled many of the kids into a doze. He could even see Carrie sleeping when he looked in the rearview mirror.

Though Carrie was a tempting sight, he hardly sneaked a peek at her, because he had to keep his wits about him while he drove the big vehicle. It would be just his luck to be watching Carrie sleep and run over an armadillo. No, it was time to keep his eyes on the road and his mind on the journey. It usually gave him quite a sense of accomplishment to drive something this big. Tonight was no different.

They might not see Texas by daylight at all on this trip. The corner that they drove through between Oklahoma and New Mexico took less than five hours to traverse, and depending on when they came back, it might be dark again, too. Not that there were that many fascinating sights along the interstate highway around Amarillo.

Carrie could probably find something interesting. So far she seemed to find the interesting and unusual everywhere she went. That surprised Rafe.

She wasn't the total flake he'd first thought her to be. True, she was high-spirited and made decisions quicker than he thought was wise. That cast was certainly an illustration of her decision-making abilities. Wouldn't most people have had the automatic self-preservation to roll into a fall instead? He knew he would have.

Cautious determination didn't seem to be the way Carrie lived life. She dived in headfirst and worried about the consequences later. The thought of being able to live that way sent chills up Rafe's spine. Still, he had to admit that Carrie's life seemed to work for her. And if she hadn't made a rash decision on the volleyball court, she wouldn't be on this trip.

And it was good having her along, despite what he'd said to Rob. He still couldn't believe his younger brother thought that he and Carrie were a couple. How did he get that idea? Carrie looked nothing like the girls Rafe had dated before. And she didn't act like them, either. Since none of those other relationships had lasted too long, maybe Rob thought Rafe was changing his ways in order to settle down.

That wasn't likely to happen anytime soon. That made two people telling him that Carrie liked him, or that they looked like a couple. And in the morning they were going to meet his opinionated sister, Renata. He could hardly wait to hear what she had to say on the matter. Of course she'd know everything before they arrived. Information tended to run through his family like wildfire.

He stole another glance back at the interior of the coach. Almost everyone seemed to be sleeping. Carrie's face had a soft glow as she slept and she looked young and vulnerable. When she wasn't challenging his sanity with some of her schemes, she was one of the most attractive women he'd ever met. For a moment he tried imagining dating Carrie Collins.

But that was impossible. Carrie might be impulsive and headstrong, but he had a feeling there was no such thing as casual dating for her. There was either plain friendship or a mad courtship that would take a man's breath away. The one kiss they'd shared had already proven that.

Rafe reached one hand out from the wheel to where his travel mug of strong coffee sat tethered in its holder. If thoughts of courting Carrie didn't demand a heavy dose of caffeine, he couldn't think of anything that did.

He drove on through the night for several hours more than he'd told Jake he would. It was good to be alone with his thoughts and his prayers, and the empty road in front of him. It gave a man time to ponder the mysteries of life. And right now one of the biggest mysteries for Rafe was how involved he was going to be with Carrie, and how involved he wanted to be.

Every mission trip he'd gone on had changed his life. Why did he have the feeling that this one would stand out as something altogether different?

Carrie liked Renata O'Connor on sight. In fact she had to admit that she was developing a fondness for the O'Connor family she'd met so far. She wasn't sure how Rafe fit into the whole picture yet. He seemed to garner everybody's respect as the successful older sibling, but at the same time catch a lot of grief from his brother and sister for his attitudes and beliefs.

It wasn't his Christian beliefs that got him in trouble with his family. They all appeared to be quite active in their faith. Rob was a pastor, and Renata's high school was a private nondenominational academy. It looked like the rest of the family took life more like the Collins family that she knew and loved. There was a lot more laughter that surrounded the rest of Rafe's family, and an easiness to Renata and Rob that she hadn't seen yet in their older brother.

True, he did seem more at ease with his family than with anyone else. But there was still a reserve about Rafe that Carrie wondered about. Why did he have to be so serious all the time? What was he afraid of? Carrie found it hard to imagine that he could be so good with the high school youth and still be so determined to be so sedate all the time. Maybe he thought he had to provide a good example for the kids.

Renata met them at the large circular drive of "her" high school, looking sharp in a black suit softened by a print blouse and a short, wavy haircut. Her hair was more the color of Rafe's, and her dark eyes resembled his, as well. There was more of a sparkle to Renata's eyes, which was one of the things that made Carrie take to her right away. The other thing that endeared her to Carrie was her ability to surprise her right off the bat. "Hi, Carrie." She greeted her first guest, smiling at Carrie's look of surprise.

"Hi. You have to be Renata, but how do you already know my name?"

Renata laughed. "Rob keeps the e-mail trail hot. I probably knew more about you by six last night than anybody on that bus does." She looked pointedly up the stairs of the coach where Rafe was standing with his clipboard. "Definitely more than at least one person on the bus, but then he's male and clueless. How was Texas?"

"Mostly dark, I have to admit. Maybe on the way back I'll be able to see more." Carrie rolled her head trying to ease the kinks out of her neck. She was so glad to be off the bus for a while. "Any chance of a few minutes' acquaintance with hot water before we have breakfast?"

"Sure. For one of Rafe's . . . mission partners . . . anything," she said, making Carrie wonder what she had originally been planning to say. "In fact I thought I'd offer anybody, kids or adults, who wanted a quick shower or change of clothes a chance to use the gym locker rooms here and freshen up in shifts. These long bus rides can get pretty uncomfortable."

"I overheard that, ma'am, and I'll take you up on a hot shower even if none of these kids do." Jake came down the stairs of the coach. "They will be showering here if they think about it twice. I understand the facilities at that orphanage in Tijuana are kind of rustic."

"Rustic? That sounds so unkind. Just think of it as summer camp with a twist." Rafe joined the group, still holding his clipboard. "I see you two women have already met. Jake, you know Carrie all too well, and the other troublemaker is my sister, Renata. And Carrie, don't believe a word of it."

"Of what?"

"Whatever my dear sister tries to tell you about my dark and shady past. It isn't true and I'll deny it to the death, especially the incident with the peppers and Tía Rosa."

"Aw, I wasn't going to tell her that one. Not on a first meeting, anyway." Renata put an arm around her brother and Carrie found herself smiling. In heels the woman

98

came very close to matching him in height. This was a family of formidable people. She found herself wondering what Rafe's parents were like, especially his mother. "I want there to be a second meeting. No sense in scaring one off that looks like a keeper."

"I'll pretend that I have no idea what you're talking about. I'm sure Carrie has no idea, either." Rafe glared at his sister, but it wasn't very effective. Carrie could tell he was aggravated, but at the same time he didn't seem to be protesting too hard.

It seemed like a good time to try and lighten the mood. "There's nothing between us, Renata. Honestly." Carrie followed the pair into the high school. "Whatever Rob told you, he was wrong. Unless he said what I just did."

Renata smiled enigmatically. "Oh, he did say just what you said. But I have to tell this slightly dense brother of mine that there *ought* to be something between you. Or at least somebody that seems as promising as you do. He's thirty years old and getting more opinionated by the minute. Time is running out for an old codger like him to find happiness. Not that he'll listen. He never listens."

"Renata, I still remember when you had skinned knees and a crush on Jimmy Davis next door. Me taking advice from you on my love life is never going to happen."

Renata's dark, wavy hair bounced when she shook her head at her brother's comments. "Come on, Carrie. I'll show you where the showers are and you can get comfortable. Then when you're done we'll take our food into the faculty lounge and visit. Maybe I *will* tell you the story about Tía Rosa and the peppers after all."

"Renata . . ." Rafe said with a warning tone in his voice.

"Oh, lighten up. She's your sister, not one of your youth group charges, Rafael. Now don't protest, because I know that's your given name. Your brother told me so. Although why anybody named you after an angel, I'll never know. Maybe you were an adorable baby."

Carrie made sure the kids were just out of hearing range. There was no sense in upsetting Rafe by letting them overhear all that. "As much as I'd like to take you up on your offer, Renata, I'm afraid I'll probably eat breakfast standing at the locker room door policing the place for water fights. But if you want to join me, that would be great."

"You're on," Renata told her. "Rafe can stand in the doorway of the boys' locker room across the gym to do the same for the guys. That way he can eavesdrop on us and make sure I don't get him into trouble."

"There's nothing you could say that would give me a different opinion of the man than I already have," Carrie told her. "Have you been down to Casa Esperanza?"

"Sure. Lots of times. It's sort of a family place. My seniors do a project every year."

"Fantastic. Let me know what I'm getting myself into there. That's the one thing your brother hasn't been very forthcoming on."

Carrie liked Renata's answering laugh. "He probably didn't want to scare you away. How do you feel about spiders?"

"They're better than snakes. I think." Carrie was almost sorry she'd started this line of questioning. She followed Renata down the hall, hoping her next question wasn't about scorpions.

Chapter Seven

After leaving Renata's high school, time seemed to blur. The second half of the trip passed quickly. Carrie ran out of ways to entertain the kids on the bus by midway through Arizona. When they finally stopped that night for a late dinner and a stretch break in Yuma, everybody was grouchy and nobody wanted to get back on the bus. Only Rafe's promise that they were less than three hours from San Diego where they would meet Pastor Garza kept the kids from mutiny. For a change Carrie could see the value of his no-nonsense approach. It got more cooperation under stress than the cajoling she would have used.

The meeting place in San Diego didn't look like much in the dark. Driving along the freeways, San Diego looked like a lovely city. Carrie was sure she'd love it in daylight. The block where Rafe instructed Jake to pull the bus over while he looked for Pastor Garza was not a special-looking place. It could have been part of any city she'd ever seen. Carrie could see what looked like a transit stop. Rafe said the pastor would be taking the trolley from Tijuana to San Diego to meet them. As they pulled over to the curb, passengers were just getting off the trolley.

One man separated himself from the throng and headed toward the bus. "Is that him?" Trent called out to Rafe.

"Sure looks like him. If he knocks on the door, we'll know, won't we?" Rafe answered back. The man obliged by coming up to the bus and knocking on the door.

"First time I've ever been cheered just for knocking," Pastor Garza said, coming aboard the coach. Even the grouchy teenagers seemed impressed by the small man who had a large presence. The pastor clapped Rafe on the shoulder, and gave Carrie the warmest handshake she'd ever gotten.

"*Los niños* are going to like this one, even with a cast," the pastor told Rafe. "The children are always interested to see who Dr. O'Connor brings with him. When I tell them that not only did he bring lots of teenagers to help build the orphanage, but also brought a pretty woman, they will not believe me. Plan on being awakened very early tomorrow, Miss Collins."

"Please just call me Carrie, Pastor. And let's get on the road so we can sleep for a while before being awakened, shall we?"

The pastor smiled in response and everyone settled into their seats. Pastor Garza took the microphone attached to Jake's sound system and started telling the youth group about Casa Esperanza and how life there would proceed for the next five days.

"Tomorrow when it gets light you can set up tents. Tonight it is too late and too dark. Plan on pitching your bedrolls between the children's bunks in the dormitory. I'm sorry there's not much space for that, but that is why you are building us a new dormitory. So that everyone can spread out a little and we can welcome more children into Casa Esperanza."

He went on to explain how breakfast would work in the morning, and where everyone could use bathrooms to get ready for the day. "I hope you have all brought your flashlights because the children will be asleep for the night before we get back, and I will not turn on our lights and wake them all up for you."

"Enough of them will sneak out of bed

anyway to come see us," Rafe said. "It always happens that way when I bring a group down to work." Carrie could imagine the amount of barely organized chaos that would meet their arrival.

She didn't have long to wonder about what would happen before other things caught her attention. First there was the border crossing from San Diego to Tijuana. That took a while as the coach was checked, everyone's documents seen to be in order as the steady line of kids trooped on and off the bus during the checks.

Finally they were back on their way again. After being on the bus for so long, it seemed a very short time before they were in Tijuana. Carrie felt as bouncy as most of the kids who were looking out the coach windows pointing out sights, wondering if their "home" for the next five days would be right around the next corner.

"Remember, our place will be a few miles out," Rafe cautioned. "I know I told everybody all of this. And Mexico is not like Missouri, where even out in the country there's a lot of lights to guide our way."

"You can say that again," Jake said, gripping the wheel like a ship's captain in a storm. "I've seen the inside of caves that were better lit than this road."

Carrie could see plenty of stars up above. She knew that wouldn't guide their driving, but it did make everything feel so peaceful. The stars looked different here, and she wondered why. Was it all because there was little electric light to compete? Or had they truly traveled far enough that even the stars were different. She made a note to ask Rafe later. He'd know what she was talking about.

Of course, if she was totally honest with herself she had to admit that they'd passed into territory where Rafe was the expert on almost everything. She'd never been farther west than the panhandle of Oklahoma in her whole life. All her Spanish, for whatever practice she'd gotten, had been spoken to people who spoke English first. She'd never crossed the border into a foreign country before.

She had plenty of experience putting up tents, and even sleeping on the ground or on hard concrete floors in a sleeping bag wasn't new to her. But Carrie had a feeling that once the building began tomorrow at Casa Esperanza, she was going to be out of her element.

A week ago, relying on Rafe as the expert

106

would have bothered her. Now she wasn't as upset by the thought. Rafe might have his drawbacks, and he was one of the most serious individuals she'd ever met. But where the children that they were coming here to help were concerned, he seemed to lighten up. Trusting Rafe to be in charge was all right with her for a change.

Rafe watched the kids listen to Jaime Garza. The group clustered in the front four rows of seats where they could hear Jaime and gave him their undivided attention, which was good. The more attention they paid to Jaime, the more interested they would be in the work in the days ahead.

He was already happy that the border crossing had gone well. Nobody had gotten out of line and messed things up for the group. It was hard convincing teenagers that what was okay, if goofy, behavior in most places just wouldn't go over well at a national border.

He checked his sheaf of paperwork to make sure that all the supplementary documents and insurance for the motor coach were in order. Five days from now he'd need it all again, and it would be easier if he could find everything on the first try.

Jaime was getting the kids excited about what they'd be doing tomorrow. "We have forty-two little girls in a building that should hold twenty-five. And we have thirty-one boys in another one that should hold no more than the girls' dormitory. So what you're doing will be appreciated the minute you finish building."

"It won't make it very easy for us to sleep tonight, will it?" Rafe could see Trent had given this some thought. Of course, at Trent's height, bunking down between the kids' beds wasn't going to be easy no matter how much room there was.

"This is true. But it's only for one night. Tomorrow you'll be in your tents instead."

"And that will be so much more comfortable, Trent," his cousin Ashleigh teased.

Trent puffed out his chest. "I can handle it. I made Eagle Scout. I can sleep on the ground a couple more nights." Ashleigh made a small face at him, and several of the youth group laughed.

"You can take comfort in the work you are doing. And because of that work, you'll probably be so tired you won't notice if you use rocks for pillows." Jaime looked out the coach window. "Can you see the lights up ahead? That is Casa Esperanza."

Listening to the kids cheer lifted Rafe's heart. This was like Christmas morning after a long wait. "I feel that way, too, just to have you here. Now remember, when you get out and unload, this place is full of sleeping children. So no loud horseplay unloading the coach. And we'll only take out what we absolutely need for tonight — bedrolls and duffels," Rafe told them all, standing in the aisle and getting ready to be a leader again. "The tents and water will wait until daylight."

"Let us do our devotions here, too, so that the children can sleep. Let us ask our Heavenly Father to bless this week ahead of us all at Casa Esperanza."

Rafe bowed his head and listened to Tío Jaime pray. He started out in English, switched over to the same phrases in Spanish, and then went back and forth a second time with a second petition. Rafe hadn't told the kids, or even Carrie, that Jaime Garza was his uncle. Carrie had already met enough of his family to be overwhelmed.

Besides, a few secrets were good. Not that his relationship with the Garzas would remain secret for long once they got into the main building at Casa Esperanza and saw Aunt Rosa. She was an older version of Renata, the resemblance so obvious that Carrie would notice right away.

Tío Jaime was done with his prayer now, and Jake pulled the bus over where Jaime told him to go. If Rafe had felt like a kid on Christmas Eve before, it was hard to describe how much anticipation was built up now.

Even though he'd never lived in Mexico, this place always made him feel like he was coming home. Perhaps it was because so much of his family had been in and around the Tijuana area all the time he was growing up.

He pushed away his private thoughts as Jake turned off the motor and the air brakes of the coach hissed. The doors swung open. It was time for him to go to work now to make sure everything went smoothly. Of course all he had to do was watch his uncle in motion. If anybody in the world could smooth over any rough situation, it was Jaime.

For a change, there were no rough situations for Jaime to handle. The unloading of the coach went quickly and quietly. The combination of Rafe's group being tired, and Jaime's warning them to be quiet, meant that things progressed in an orderly fashion.

He felt very proud of this bunch of kids. He was proud of Carrie, too. When Tía Rosa came out of the main building and hugged him, and hugged Carrie after introductions were made, Carrie's eyebrows went up. She looked at him in a way that told Rafe there would be much conversation later. But for now she just greeted his aunt and followed her to the girls' dormitory where she would spend the night.

Carrie was anxious to see Casa Esperanza in the light. Everything smelled warm and fragrant, as if they were surrounded by flowering plants. They weren't smells of plants she could identify at home, but they smelled wonderful. The buildings were pale in the wan moonlight, but she couldn't tell much about them besides their shape and general size when all their light came from small flashlights.

Rafe's excitement at being here was contagious. If she hadn't been so tired, she would have wanted to sit with the rest of the adults and talk until dawn. And the first thing she would have figured out from Rosa and Jaime was how Rafe was related to them. Even by flashlight Carrie could see that Rosa was a darker, slightly older-looking version of Renata. It made her wonder what Rafe's parents looked like.

It miffed her a little that he hadn't bothered to mention his relationship with the Garzas with her. But Rafe didn't share much of his personal life with anybody. Carrie didn't have time to dwell on that before they'd reached the doorway of the girls' dormitory.

Rosa explained the layout of the rooms to everyone before they went in. The girls nodded sleepily while Carrie and Rosa sorted them out into twos and threes to bed down between sets of bunks. Rosa directed each group through the door and pointed them to a place between bunks. Once they spread out sleeping bags or bedrolls on the smooth concrete floor, they headed in the same small groups into the washroom to get ready for bed.

When it was Carrie's turn for the washroom she looked around, thinking she hadn't seen anything quite like it before. From what Rafe said, she knew this was a luxury for the kids who lived here. Washing her face in a basin by flashlight set up on a shelf, casting shadows on the cinder-block walls, she breathed a silent prayer for all the things in her apartment at home that she took for granted every day.

Why hadn't she ever thought about how great warm, running water was before? And lights that flicked on when you touched them, and pretty, soft towels by the dozens? She lit her way back to bed with her small flashlight, listening to children sigh and whisper in the dark. Stretched out in her sleeping bag she breathed a silent prayer and closed her eyes. Morning would come quickly and she needed all the sleep she could get.

Before her eyes opened all the way in the daylight and she could focus, Carrie heard voices. There were tiny, little-girl voices whispering and giggling in Spanish. Then there were the slightly deeper teenage voices giggling and whispering in English.

The quiet intensity made her wonder what she was going to see when she actually opened her eyes. Had the girls played some kind of prank on her while she slept?

She peeked out of her sleeping bag while doing a physical check of the surrounding space with her hands. No shaving cream or other foreign substances had been spread around the area. That was good news.

Directly in her line of vision was the most beautiful little girl she'd ever seen. Her brown face broke into a smile of pure joy when Carrie looked at her. Chocolate eyes even darker than Rafe's sparkled in a round-cheeked face. A halo of soft curls even a shade darker than her eyes framed her sweet smile. Carrie didn't know enough about little kids to guess her age accurately. She was too old to be a toddler, but didn't look old enough for grade school.

"Hi. *Hola. Buenos días.*" "Hello" and "Good morning" were the only phrases Carrie could dredge up before she'd gotten more awake. The girl smiled even wider, but didn't say anything back. Carrie wondered if she was shy, or just didn't understand her Spanish. She waved at her to see if she could get a response from the gesture.

The little girl wiggled tentative fingers in return. "My name is Carrie. What's yours?" Carrie asked in Spanish. Or at least she hoped she did. Words were still an effort this morning as she sat up and stretched.

The little girl cocked her head, looking slightly puzzled. Everybody around them seemed to be watching the exchange and giggling a little. "Hey, Carrie, I don't think she'll talk to you. She wouldn't talk to any of us, and the other girls are trying to tell us something about her." Ashleigh was dressed in shorts and a clean shirt already, and sat down on the edge of the nearest bunk.

"I think her name is Lucia. And the others keep trying to tell us Lucia is *muda*. What does that mean?"

Carrie's heart sank while she looked at the beautiful child in front of her. "I'm not positive, but I think I have an idea." She looked around the room and found the biggest girl who was awake and visiting with the American contingent. Carrie would have guessed her for ten or eleven, and she motioned her over. She managed to establish that the older girl was Elisa, and that Lucia was her beautiful companion's name. *"¿Lucia no hablar?"* she asked the older girl, only to have her confirm what she was afraid of. Her beautiful new friend, Lucia, with the smile that lit the room, could not speak.

So for the rest of her morning Carrie had a silent shadow. Lucia followed her into the bathroom, solemnly watching her wash her face. She had already gotten dressed and ready for the day before Carrie got up, or someone had helped her. She wore a simple little dress and cheap rubber sandals, but they were clean and neat like all the other girls.

Her quiet among the chatter around her was almost unnerving. Lucia didn't seem to be unhappy or bothered by anything. Carrie's spitting toothpaste in the sink made her giggle without noise, making Carrie consider brushing her teeth twice just for the reaction. But she knew water was precious as was time this morning, so in the end she took Lucia's hand and went back out into the main room instead.

Most of her teenage charges were already up and moving. Bedrolls were being stacked against the outside walls, and duffel bags were zipped up and ready to move when the tents would be put up. Carrie hoped that would be after breakfast and devotions. She needed a little more time to feel human again before she started challenging things like putting up tents.

Of course it was a little silly to put them up right away when no one was going to use them until nightfall, she reasoned. Maybe they'd go straight into building the additions before putting up their own tents. Looking out the one window nearby, she could see that it was a clear, sunny morning. And she could tell it was already warm.

She wondered if Rafe had got his

morning coffee. Now that she knew that Rosa and Jaime were some kind of extended family, she suspected that he would. The O'Connors, even when they were teasing, seemed to look out for each other very well. This branch of the family wouldn't be much different, she suspected.

Once she zipped up her own duffel and slipped her tennis shoes on, there was a small hand in hers again. There was something almost heartbreaking about Lucia's attachment to her. She wished she knew more about her and what kept her from speaking. For now she had to settle for the child's soft hand in hers, leading her across the flat dusty yard into the main building where Rafe and breakfast waited.

When they got there, Rafe was sitting at one of the long tables, surrounded by boys and young men of all sizes. He was sipping something out of a mug and looking happy.

"Café con leche," he told her in way of greeting. "Coffee with milk. My aunt Rosa makes the best, and she has assured me she wasn't depriving anybody by giving me a cup. Go in and help yourself, if she'll let you."

"Good morning to you, too," Carrie said, trying not to sound tart. "I see you're doing your part to conserve water."

Rafe ran a hand over his chin. "I don't usually shave on these trips. It gives me another ten minutes to sleep before getting up at dawn and starting the day. Who's your friend?"

"Her name is Lucia. She's . . ." Carrie stalled a moment, trying to decide how much to tell him, and how.

Rafe solved her problem. "Tía Rosa told me about her. She likes you, doesn't she?"

"I hope so. She seems to have decided I need taking care of." Carrie let herself be led into the kitchen, where Rosa was handing out glasses of milk and plates of tortillas and sweet pastries.

"Good morning. I hope you slept well," Rosa said. "I see Lucia has found you."

"She's beautiful. And Elisa has already told me about her."

"That she does not speak? It is one of our sorrows. We hope Rafael can do something for her when he goes back to his hospital. But for now she is cheerful most of the time, and beautiful, no? And she will be happy to have sweet *buñuelos* for breakfast to celebrate your coming."

The love Rosa had for all the children was evident in the way she greeted them and served each one breakfast. And Lucia did seem happy to have breakfast while sitting next to Carrie in the dining room. Her legs swung like any little girl's as she sipped her milk and Carrie drank her coffee.

They'd just met and still Carrie was so deeply in love with this little child she could hardly stand it. Yesterday she didn't understand how her sisters felt toward their children. Today she knew, and it terrified her.

Chapter Eight

By nine in the morning Carrie understood why they only brought T-shirts and shorts along. She was dripping with sweat and covered with dust and the sun wasn't anywhere near its worst. She kept reminding the kids to drink water, even before they were thirsty.

"This isn't like back home in Missouri where the heat feels steamy. It's drier here, and you can really dehydrate quickly." She made sure to take her own advice. It wasn't particularly comfortable wearing the cast, and she knew that just dragging it around probably made her use more water than normal. It definitely felt like she was sweating even more than usual under the plaster on her arm.

Jake and Letty stopped in to tell everyone goodbye until Friday. They were going back to San Diego to take in the sights for a few days. "We'll have a second honeymoon," Letty said. "Never did get around to that first one and it's been eight years."

"Since what?" Carrie asked.

"Since the first one," Jake told her. Her surprise was evident in his answering laugh. "Of course you probably had us pegged for working on our golden wedding anniversary, didn't you?"

"Honestly, I did. Of course that's foolish of me. My own father hasn't even gotten to his first anniversary yet on his second time around, and he's . . ." Carrie stopped when she realized what she was going to say.

"Younger than we are?" Letty filled in, grinning while she said it. "That's all right. He probably is. We are having a grand time, no matter if there's snow on the roof. And still being able to do something like driving this bus, while being together is more fun."

"Well, have a good time in San Diego and we'll see you at the end of the week. Rosa and Jaime will help keep the teens in line while you're gone," Rafe said. "Drive carefully, now."

"Oh, don't worry," Letty told him. "Once we get to the motel in San Diego we're renting a little two-seater convertible and hopping around in that all week. Taking a thirty-passenger coach on vacation isn't my idea of a good time, even with Jake along."

Laughter and goodbyes followed them as they got into the coach and drove away. The little children all waved, and Jake blew the horn for them. That brought Pastor Garza out to watch the commotion. He went back into the main building when the bus pulled away.

"Probably going over the books," Rafe said. "That or the plans for what we're building, trying to see if we've really got all the materials we need for the week."

"And if we don't?" Carrie felt foolish as soon as she asked.

"Then we work with what we have for as long as it lasts and pray until the rest comes in. But knowing Uncle Jaime, he's done plenty of that already."

Carrie was happy to be in the company of a man who was that matter-of-fact about faith and prayer. She'd met too many cynical guys through Fire and Rescue. It was good to be keeping company with somebody that was comfortable with both hard work and the power of prayer.

She must have been looking at Rafe too fondly, because he suddenly seemed to scowl. Rafe looked around at the crew sitting on the ground, drinking water. "Okay, break time is over. Who wants their first lesson in building with concrete block? Come over to the corner of the footings poured for us and we'll get started."

Carrie went over to listen with the kids. At this stage of the project she was learning along with them. Until they started hammering nails or painting walls, building was completely foreign territory to her. It was also difficult to do with one arm in a cast. She looked around at the diverse crew around her. Were they really going to build something people could live in?

Of course Carrie's shadow had followed her. Lucia had slipped out of the building sometime earlier and hung on the edge of the group. Now when Carrie sat with the others on the concrete foundation pad to listen to Rafe explain the plans for the day, Lucia sat next to her. And as she settled in, Carrie felt a small hand on her knee, resting there in a companionable fashion. It made contemplating hauling concrete blocks much easier to have that small hand on her knee. Carrie breathed a silent prayer of thanks for that soft, small hand, patted it and went on listening.

Lunch was a welcome break, eaten in the cool dining room with the children. Many of the older boys and girls were at school. But the little ones were present. They looked over the youth group's peanut butter or turkey sandwiches a little warily before trying them. Rosa explained that they didn't have American-style food very often unless they had visitors.

Once everyone was seated with food in front of them, Carrie found herself next to Rosa at the table. Lucia was nearby, with another slightly older little girl who appeared to take charge of her during meals. "So tell me about my small friend," Carrie said, motioning toward Lucia.

"I can tell you as much as we know. It isn't everything. There are few of these children we know everything about. Only God knows all of each child's past." Rosa spoke matter-of-factly.

She looked down the table, seeming to gather her thoughts for a moment. "Lucia was a little over three when she came to us. We think she was born speaking, then lost the ability or the will as a little one. She does not speak, but she laughs once in a while. And we know she hears."

"Good. How did she come here? Did she have any family?"

"She has a mother, and there's a father somewhere. He went north to find work when Lucia was a baby, and he didn't send money or come back. It is a familiar story here." Rosa sighed and reached across the table to help a child with lunch. Once that was done, she continued her story.

"Lucia's mother was very young. She gave her heart to a young man who had no intention of marriage. So she had no husband, little family and no job skills. Like many women in her situation, she fell on the wrong side of the law. When she was arrested and put in prison, she had two choices — she could abandon her little girl to the streets or take her with her."

"To prison?" Carrie couldn't imagine it. Even the clean, relatively calm conditions of an American jail weren't somewhere you'd bring a child. What she'd seen of Tijuana didn't make a prison sound like the right place for an adult, much less a child.

"When there is no family 'outside' to care for the little ones, often they go to prison with their mothers. This is changing, but not fast enough."

"What will happen to Lucia when her mother gets out?" Carrie watched the little girl smiling with her friend, sharing an apple between the two of them.

"Nothing different. When we came to

the prison to get the child, her mother signed over her rights to Lucia. She is ours now. I don't think her mother saw a future where she could raise a child, especially one with problems. Some days I wonder myself what will become of her."

Rosa's pronouncement made Carrie tear up. She could hardly bear to consider this beautiful little girl's future. Lucia was a sweet, friendly child. Her happiness should be assured, like any of God's children here or elsewhere. What kind of a world had they built where that wasn't the case?

Carrie looked down at her plate, considering the half-eaten sandwich there. She didn't have much appetite for it any more, but she needed to eat. Today food was merely strength for the project, and it would be a long and arduous day.

During the afternoon, when any normal person would have been taking a siesta, the youth group put up their tents. It was cooler work than building with concrete block, but then anything would have been. They all took turns raising the four- to six-person nylon tents and sitting in the shade, moving as little as possible.

Trent and Ashleigh, oddly enough, made one of the best tent-raising teams. Even though their height differed by nearly a foot, they communicated well enough to get the complicated arrangements of poles, nylon walls and tie-down strings to work together. Carrie almost felt jealous of the duo. If she had the use of both arms, she would be helping putting up tents. Instead, she supervised one of the groups, consisting of Heather, Missy and two of their friends, as they struggled with their own tent. It wasn't a pretty picture.

"Missy, you should know more about this. After all, it's your tent." Heather pushed limp wet hair away from her face. "Why can't we get it to stay up straight?"

"I don't know. It's not like I ever put it up before or anything. And it's not my tent anyway, it's my brother Chad's tent that they use for Boy Scout camping trips."

"So? You should still know how to do this. It's your family's tent, anyway." Heather looked about ready to give the one standing pole a good swift kick.

Carrie couldn't stay out of the discussion any longer. "Okay, you two. This is not cooperation. And I know we don't have any instructions for putting up this tent. But surely a resourceful bunch like you can figure this out." They actually nodded and started to do just that, to Carrie's amazement.

"Nice work," a deep voice murmured behind her. "You can do good things with these kids. Think of what you could accomplish with two hands free."

She turned to face Rafe, who looked as hot and bedraggled as she did. It surprised her that he also looked dashing at the same time. There was a smudge of dirt on one cheek, and his shirt looked like it had been through the wringer, but it all suited him. She raised her right arm, complete with cast, to his eye level. "Oh, I do think of it, Dr. O'Connor. Quite often. Of course my attending physician didn't leave me an option."

He eased her arm down gently. "But if he had, would you be here? You're the one that told me that God works in strange ways sometimes. And I really am beginning to believe you. This might be the most fun I've ever had on one of these trips, and we're still getting plenty done."

Was that a compliment? From Rafe? Would wonders never cease? "You know, you might not be as bad to get along with as I thought you were, O'Connor. I still think we should have made room in the luggage for a few more water guns. Look how handy they would have come in today."

Rafe shook his head. "No deal. Just because I said you might be right on some things doesn't mean I want this turned into a free-for-all. Besides, Tía Rosa doesn't allow toy weapons, even neon-colored water guns. These kids have seen too much of that already."

Carrie winced. "I hadn't thought about things that way. Maybe I can come up with some kind of water system that doesn't involve firearms. These kids could use more fun in their lives."

Rafe shrugged. "According to you, everybody could use more fun in their lives. And like I said, you may have a point. Just remember there's things they need even more than fun, like a new place to sleep."

"I can't lose sight of that. Especially not with my constant companion." Carrie motioned toward Lucia, who was sitting against the wall with some of the older girls, sharing a drink of water. "She needs a place to sleep, and a whole lot more. How come there's no medical clinic for these kids?"

"No money. No town. No doctor crazy enough." Rafe's voice got flatter with every pronouncement. "And if you are about to say that I'm just the guy for that job, leave it right there, because I don't agree." With that he turned and went back to his own tent setup.

"Guess he said his piece," she muttered as she went back to setting up the tent with the girls.

Heather heard her, because the slight girl shook her head. "Don't get too upset, Carrie. You know why he's so crabby with you, don't you?"

Missy sidled over to her friend. "Heather, why don't we work on the pegs over on the other side? I think we're ready to go."

"No, this pole needs more work. Besides, I was talking to Carrie."

"I know." Missy was trying hard to communicate something to Heather. "And maybe now isn't the time to talk about that."

"Why not? You were the one who said . . ." Heather started, only to have Missy dump the contents of her carry-along water bottle over her head. Squealing ensued and Carrie had to wade in between them to prevent general chaos. Once she was done stopping the friendly battle, she had to admit that maybe Rafe had a point about water guns, water fights and water play in general. But breaking up the melee left her the coolest and most comfortable she'd felt all morning.

Rafe felt as if his head were going to explode. Whatever had possessed him to answer Carrie that way? She didn't know the first thing about his personal situation, or the number of times that Rosa and Jaime had hinted that he could be of great help setting up medical care for the kids. He'd really overreacted to an innocent suggestion on her part.

Not that her concern ought to be a surprise. He'd guessed that once she'd met Jaime and Rosa's kids, she would care for every one of them. He knew she was falling for Lucia. And seeing the little girl with Carrie tugged at his own heartstrings. She was right about Lucia; the child needed far more medical care than she was going to get here unless somebody intervened. And he knew who that "somebody" probably needed to be. But today he couldn't spend the time thinking about it. He was going to get the tents up, have a short Bible study with these kids until it got just a little cooler, then put up at least two more courses of concrete block.

If he still had any brain cells left to deal with complicated problems after all of that, maybe he could give the medical situation at Casa Esperanza some thought. That wasn't very likely to be the case, though.

By nightfall he'd proved himself right. At least there wasn't going to be a problem with the kids acting up and getting into trouble. Most of them were so tired they were having trouble staying awake during dinner. He saw more than one person at the supper table who seemed to be propped up on their elbows just to stay upright and get a fork into their mouth.

Carrie was just as bad as the kids, especially since she only had one elbow capable of being used for propping herself. She had finally resorted to a sling around her cast for dinner. "Heavy?" he asked, motioning across the table.

"As lead. And that was just the least of my problems. However, I could fix it, so I did."

"You've got problems you can't fix?"

"Not major ones, I guess. But showering or bathing with a garbage bag over one arm is the worst. And I haven't yet found a way to wash my hair with one hand. For the first time in years I really regret having hair this long."

"Sorry to hear that. Because your hair is one of my favorite things about you. Especially when you wear it in a ponytail like that."

"Yeah, well, I seem to remember that made you think I was a high school kid when you were looking at my arm."

Rosa was sitting at their end of the table, and her eyebrow went up in a disbelieving arch. "Did you really? If this is true, I worry about you, Rafael."

"Then worry about him, because in the emergency room he asked me where my mom or dad was." Her answer made Rafe wince. It wasn't the kind of story he wanted to share with his aunt. He'd certainly hear about this for years.

"I hope you corrected him quickly." Rosa was smiling broadly. "And often. He isn't the most social person. Not that his mother didn't try her best to make him a gentleman."

"Mama did very well. I just lost a few of my polished edges someplace. Probably medical school." Rafe quickly thought of something to say to lead the conversation onto another topic. "But Carrie isn't used to polite doctors, anyway. She works for the county Fire and Rescue service, so she knows all about rude hospital people."

Rosa brightened even more. "So you, too, have medical knowledge. Perhaps if the building gets too difficult with one arm, you can teach me a few things I need to know. Since we do not have a doctor or a clinic nearby, it gets difficult at times."

Good job, man. He'd managed to go from the frying pan into the fire. "I've noticed that," Carrie piped up before Rafe could switch to another topic. You could count on these women to stick together. "And I'd be happy to do what I can. I've got my paramedic and EMT training. Not nearly as much medical experience as Rafe, but I could be of help."

"Good. And in return I could get the girls to wash your hair. They would have fun playing with it. It's such a lovely color. Don't you think so, Rafael?" Rosa looked at him, daring him to say anything to the contrary.

"Lovely, Tía Rosa. Now what can we do to help clean up after dinner until it's time for a campfire and putting this worn-out bunch to bed?"

Rosa shook her head. "There is a reason we ate off of paper plates. That way the children who have kitchen duty will need very little help past their normal chores. And then the older ones can join you at your campfire, if it is all right with you. They are always happy to have you around."

"Sure. It will give my kids a chance to practice their Spanish and yours to practice their English. Everybody benefits."

"True. Other than me, who will lose my helpers for putting the little ones to bed. But the older ones deserve this kind of treat when they can find it."

"And I can help you put kids to bed," Carrie told her. That won her major brownie points with Rafe. She didn't strike him as the domestic type, but she was always surprising him. "I enjoy singing lullabies. And I have a feeling I'll have lots of help any time I need to do anything that takes two hands." She looked down the table and all their gazes went in the same direction.

"Lucia. She doesn't normally attach herself to strangers, you know. You should consider yourself special, Carrie. But then, if you kept better company than my socially inept nephew, you already would."

Rosa got up to clear the table, leaving Rafe dumbfounded. His family was really ganging up on him.

Chapter Nine

By the middle of Wednesday afternoon the concrete block walls of the new addition to Casa Esperanza were as tall as Carrie. There were window frames in several places to give the building light, and doorways that led both to the outside and to the main building, in accordance with Pastor Garza's plan. It amazed her that this group of novice builders could put together a real building.

Of course they had Jaime, Rosa and Rafe to rely on, and all of them had been a part of the process before. But normally the kids could barely function as a team for simple things at church. For them to be able to create a building that was almost ready for a roof was beyond Carrie's understanding.

Carrie knew the credit for most of this had to go to God, with a helping hand from Rafe and his aunt and uncle. The more she saw Rafe and Jaime working together, the more she wondered about

Rafe's parents. He and Jaime functioned as a team, better than most fathers and sons. And Rosa clucked over him as well as any mother Carrie had ever seen.

But where were his real parents? Why hadn't they contacted them? Rafe had planned his trip in such a way to touch base with both his brother and sister. In their brief conversations, all of them had mentioned San Diego being home during their teen years. But none of them had talked about their parents very much.

All of that made Carrie wonder what was the reason for Rafe not spending any time in San Diego, where he'd mentioned going to high school and college. If visiting Rob and Renata was important, why not his family in San Diego? Carrie wondered about Rafe's family for most of the day while she helped lay courses of concrete block.

She wondered about it even more when Rosa pulled her aside during the heat of the afternoon and told her to come inside. It was on the tip of her tongue to ask about Rafe's parents while they went over medical records together.

Carrie read through the various forms that Rosa put before her and explained what she could of each child's medical history, as it was sketched out in the records at Casa Esperanza. Most of the time Rosa had to translate things for her, because Carrie's knowledge of Spanish didn't include a lot of more complicated medical terms. So Carrie felt like they were helping each other; Rosa was teaching her more Spanish and Carrie was teaching her medical terms.

When they went over the various problems these children had faced in their short lives, Rafe's family problems, if he even had any, paled in comparison. After an hour or so, Carrie had so many questions she wanted to ask Rosa about the kids, that Rafe's family situation had faded from her mind.

It had only taken an hour reading files to see that for most of Casa Esperanza's kids, Jaime and Rosa were the end of the road in one sense, the beginning of life in another. They had been taken in, sheltered, clothed and loved, often for the first time in their lives. Most of them had been anywhere from four days old to eight years old when they entered the Casa.

By four in the afternoon Carrie felt as if she'd spent the entire time continuing to haul concrete blocks. "How can you do what you do?" she finally asked Rosa. The question had burned a path through Carrie's brain. "There's no money for anything, yet you have over seventy children here and you take care of them. It doesn't even begin to make sense."

"If you're looking for things that make sense, you've come to the wrong place." Rosa smiled as she said it. "I don't need to make sense of how God works in this place. That part I will never understand. All I need to understand is some of these medical things about my children. Obviously, that is part of the reason you have been brought here."

"It sure wasn't to build that addition. I feel like I haven't been much help there at all." Carrie felt frustrated by her own uselessness.

Rosa waved away her concerns. "Rafael and Jaime have all those strong, young bodies to do that. I had hoped that Rafael would have time to look at these things in the evenings and talk to me, but he is so tired. He puts his whole heart into this place."

"He puts his whole heart into his work, period." Carrie found the truth of him as the words came out of her mouth. "That describes him, doesn't it? I've been trying to figure out what makes him so different from most people I know. And especially what makes him different from Rob and Renata. And that's it. He pours his whole heart into his work."

"While they keep some of their heart for others? You're right. He's been that way since he was very young." Rosa took a long look at Carrie. "How much has he told you about his family?"

"Nothing. I only know what I've seen before we got here. He didn't even tell me that you and Pastor Garza were related to him. I still don't know exactly how you're related, just that he calls you 'Aunt' and 'Uncle.'"

"I am Rafael's mother's sister. My only sister, Cruz, was younger by four years. She was the light of everyone's life, always happy and cheerful. She went to the United States to go to nursing school, and graduated with honors. She worked in a hospital in Texas where she met an American doctor named Russell O'Connor."

"Had she planned to come back to Mexico to be a nurse?"

"Yes, but that all changed when she met Russell. They fell in love and were quickly married. They were very happy, and God blessed them with children. In five years there were three babies, and Cruz stopped working as a nurse."

"Were they still living in Texas? Did they visit you often?"

"When the children were very small, they still lived in Texas. But Russell could see how much Cruz missed her family. We were close, but none of us could afford to come to Texas to visit very often, and traveling with three little children was hard for Cruz. So they moved to San Diego, where she could see her family in Baja, California, quite often."

Rosa smiled. "Do you really want to know all of this? I have no one to talk to about family things most of the time."

"I'm enjoying it. Please, go on. I noticed you have said 'was' when you talk about Rafe's mother. Is she no longer living?"

"Six years ago she died. She had heart trouble, of a serious nature which she did not share with the rest of us. I think that not even Russell knew everything. I believe Rafael somehow blames his father for her death. I know it has caused discomfort between them." Rosa sighed.

Carrie tried to imagine how she would have felt if she thought her father was responsible in any way for her mother's death. But she just couldn't put herself in Rafe's place. In her family her father had

141

been the rock everyone had leaned on when her mother was ill. "Has his father ever remarried?"

"No. I think for Russell, Cruz was also his light, as she was for us. When that light went out, he did not think to replace it."

Carrie sat silently with Rosa, thinking about everything she had said. She wished that Rafe had told her even a small part of this himself. Knowing all this made her understand a little better why he seemed so focused on one thing at a time. And she was beginning to see why he kept a distance between himself and others. She didn't agree with it, but she at least could understand it.

"Have I said so much that you are speechless?" Rosa asked tentatively. She had what looked like an uneasy smile on her face.

"No, just thinking. Rafe and I have much in common, but at the same time we've handled our lives so differently. My mother is dead, also. She had a long battle with cancer, and she died when I was a teenager. My father has just remarried, and I'm very happy for him. His new wife, Gloria, is probably the reason he's still alive."

"Happiness in life makes us all live

longer, I think," Rosa said.

"So does being married to a woman who insists you go to the hospital when you're having a heart attack," Carrie said. "And in my father's case that is what kept him alive."

"Ah. There is quite a bit that you could share with my nephew. If he would let you." Rosa didn't say anything else. She didn't need to. Carrie had seen enough of the self-sufficient Rafe O'Connor to understand what she meant.

Seeing Carrie and Rosa sitting at Rosa's desk in the kitchen of the big main building with that many files and papers spread out between them made Rafe break out into a cold sweat. He could tell they'd been talking for a long time, and he knew that with these two women, the children of Casa Esperanza hadn't been their only topic of conversation.

"So, do you now know all my deep, dark secrets?" Rafe said, trying to sound a lot more jovial than he felt.

"Some of them, maybe. Probably no more than you know about me from hanging around Trent and Jeremy." Carrie didn't look at him like he had two heads, so maybe Rosa hadn't said much. "And now your Tía Rosa knows a lot more about some of her kids' medical problems. Although neither of us learned anything more about Lucia."

"That's a shame. What's holding you back?" He liked the little girl, and felt genuinely sorry for her. He hadn't told Carrie how much he hoped that her problem was purely physical, or how sure he was that it *wasn't* just an easily fixed glitch of some kind in her vocal cords that led to her silence.

"The presence of a decent children's hospital between here and San Diego, for one thing. A couple minor details like money, health insurance and an international border. But other than that . . ." Carrie's nose wrinkled when she described it all. The depth of feeling she showed for this child she'd known three days made Rafe want to grab her and kiss her senseless. "So, did you come in here for a reason or did you just think I'd been talking with your aunt too long?"

She was cute, but way too perceptive. "Maybe a little of both. We need another set of hands, or at least what you can provide. And I did want to make sure Tía left some of my past untouched."

Rosa got up from her seat at the desk

and waved dismissively. "Men. They are always so sure we talk about them. As if there is nothing more exciting in the world."

"And there is?" He knew that would get them both going.

"Sure. Kids, shoe shopping, soap operas, anything." Carrie had a broad grin now. "Isn't that right?"

"Never. Neither of you strikes me as shoe shoppers, unless it would be for that mob just coming home from school. They've got to set you back an incredible amount for shoes."

"We get many donations at just the right time." Rosa made it sound like sheer Providence. She didn't say how many hours she spent in prayer telling the Lord exactly what size and color shoes each child needed while she was doing chores around the home. "But if they are home from school I need to get busy again."

"And so do I. What did you need a hand with? Literally." Carrie waved her good hand around.

"Jaime's one complicated piece of work on the building is the fit of the roof trusses on top of the concrete block walls. It's going to take all the bigger guys up on ladders and struts, and everybody else down below pulling on ropes to get things settled. Even you."

"Oh, joy. More sweat under my cast. And here I'd finally gotten two whole hours together where I didn't want to jam something down there and scratch."

"You know what your doctor said about that."

"Yeah, and you know what he can do about it . . ." Carrie's expression told him everything he needed to know about that idea. He was beginning to be able to read her looks and gestures. Some of them he liked. Others, like this, scared him silly because they drew him closer to this mercurial woman. And growing closer to any woman made Rafe very nervous.

Two hours later there wasn't enough property in Casa Esperanza to contain him and Carrie Collins at the same time. They weren't the only ones expressing displeasure at each other, either. Looking down at the teen girls and the boys on the ground, Rafe had to admit that trying to tackle the roof trusses this late in the day had been a mistake.

It was precise work that took a lot of communication to get each truss tied in exactly where it needed to be. Jaime had a talent for it, but the rest of them faltered badly. There had been plenty of bruised feelings and fingers in the sweltering late-afternoon heat.

It was up to him to solve the problem. As usual. Rafe took a deep breath. "Okay, let's get this one done and call it a day," he said, looking around at his grouchy crew. "We've pushed ourselves too far, and it's my fault."

His admission appeared to surprise those around him. "Gee, what happened to 'We can get them all done before dark'?" Carrie snapped. "Did you decide we weren't competing in the Ironman building contest after all?"

"Yeah, I did. And I should have decided that about an hour ago. I just got carried away thinking about getting it all done."

Jaime mopped his brow with a faded-blue bandanna. "I was wondering when you'd come to that decision. I would have quit three rows ago and been happy with being halfway done. There is always another day tomorrow, you know."

"Yeah, but I want this whole thing done before we leave." Rafe knew he sounded like a whiny kid. "It will give everybody so much more sense of accomplishment."

Carrie chuckled. "You mean, it's what

was on *your* master plan, and you want the sense of accomplishment."

"You were in there with Tía Rosa way, way too long." He reached for the ladder and eased down to the ground. It wasn't an easy climb after two hours up on the joists tying things down. Every muscle screamed at the punishment he'd inflicted on his body.

"I don't think I was there long enough. I didn't get to ask her where you get this maniac streak. Although I'm sure it has something to do with your medical training. Every doctor I've worked with seems to exhibit it at some point."

"Yeah, that's just the sort of ambulance-jockey comment I'd expect from you," Rafe said, then nearly gasped at the flash of hot anger he'd provoked in Carrie's blue eyes. Ouch. This was one time even he could see where he'd overstepped the line.

"Whoa. I'm terribly sorry for what I just said, and I'm asking you to forgive that crack." He looked around at the wide-eyed teenagers on the ground around them. "See, guys, this is what a real man does when he screws up."

Feeling light-headed and clownish, he got down on one knee. "Ah, fair maid, I have wronged thee. Tell me how I can make amends."

Carrie's eyes widened in astonishment. Maybe he was just too close to her, holding her hand in his.

"Apology accepted, I think. But you're not getting off that lightly." She took her fingertips back, resting them on one cheek in thought. "Actually, there is something you can do for me if you want to make amends."

"Sure. Anything." Still down on one knee, Rafe found he meant it.

"Wash my hair. I haven't been able to do it right since we got here and Rosa hadn't had a chance to get her girls to wash it."

"Certainly. Show me where you keep the shampoo." Rafe knew he'd regret this. Especially with the hooting crowd he was going to attract from the youth group. But he'd gone too far to back down now.

Word spread quickly about his penance, and not only the youth group gathered, but most of the resident kids as well, in the side courtyard. Rafe chose an older boy, Juan, to help him. They dragged a chair and a small table out, and a plastic dishpan. Towels came from several directions, and more bottles of shampoo than Rafe thought the whole female half of the youth group possessed ranged on the table.

Juan informed Rafe that hot water was on its way as he looked at the different bottles. "So are you more of a kiwi-strawberry kind of girl, or chamomile-lemongrass?"

Carrie groaned. "I usually go for whatever is on sale. Just pick one and get to work before the audience grows any bigger."

There was quite a crowd. Rafe had never washed anybody else's hair before. He felt a little awkward doing it here with this many spectators. While he waited for the hot water, he made sure Carrie was well draped in towels and had a plastic bag to protect her cast, and that she was comfortable leaning back over the basin.

"So go ahead and dump some of that water," Missy told him. "It's not like it's ice-cold or anything." Rafe put his fingers in the bucket of water. Missy was right. He'd been part of civilization in the north so long he'd forgotten that most places don't have the luxury of cold tap water. Dipping a plastic cup into the bucket, he leaned Carrie's head back over the basin and wet down her head.

A green bottle of shampoo caught his eye, looking like the perfect contrast to her red hair. He squeezed out a bit of the liquid, which smelled like something you'd put on a salad. Now what? He tried to think about washing his own hair in the shower, but that wasn't anything like this. His short hair didn't have a mind of its own, wrapping around his wrists and fingers.

"Lather. Rinse. Repeat. The directions are on the bottle, O'Connor," Carrie forced out between clenched teeth. "Please. I'm getting a kink in my neck."

Looking down at her, Rafe could tell that wasn't where her discomfort was coming from. Carrie's face was covered with a fine sheen of perspiration that made her look as uncomfortable as he felt. And it had nothing to do with a kink in her neck.

As he rinsed the first round of lather out of her hair with the warmer water little Juan provided, Rafe tried to moisten his lips. It was a lost battle. Why hadn't anybody warned them about how incredibly intimate this act would be? His fingers tingled, buried deep in Carrie's damp hair. And he couldn't do a thing about the feelings this whole experience was bringing to the surface, waves of heat that made him feel warmer than he'd been on the roof of the building.

"Rafael?" Carrie's eyes were open, looking up at him with the same intensity he knew was reflected in his own. Her voice got even quieter. "I am so sorry I asked you to do this. It should have been something easy, like brain surgery."

"You feel it, too?" He worked up the second head of lather, trying to get this over with quickly without pulling her hair.

"Oh, yeah." Carrie closed her eyes. He could hear the low noise in her throat that he was sure would have been a full-fledged moan of pleasure if their audience hadn't numbered in the dozens.

If it wouldn't have provoked the water fight of the century, he would have upended the bucket over her just to break the tension. But after all his preaching to her about decorum, Rafe knew Carrie would kill him if he pulled that stunt. So he quietly and quickly rinsed her hair again, then helped her wrap a towel around it.

He thought the tension between them would ease when they were both standing upright and facing each other again. Instead it was just as intense as when his hands were tangled in her auburn mane.

He had to either say something or kiss her senseless. "So tell me I'm forgiven."

"Before the first rinse. You will never cease to amaze me, O'Connor." Without another word Carrie headed for the sea of tents. Watching her retreat Rafe thought to himself how he felt exactly the same way about her.

Chapter Ten

There had to be a rock under her sleeping bag. That was the only explanation Carrie could think of for why her exhausted body wouldn't go to sleep. After the day she'd had, nothing should be keeping her from sleep.

No, after the day she'd had, she would be a fool to expect her body to sleep. On the other side of the tent her teenage companions hadn't moved in an hour. Their labors had exhausted them to the point that an earthquake probably wouldn't rouse them.

Glad she'd stayed fully dressed in the day's shorts and shirt, Carrie slipped out of the tent to look at the night sky. She transferred her shower sandals from one hand to her feet as silently as possible and picked her way through the courtyard field of tents.

She thought about scratching on the flap of Rafe's tent to see if he was as awake as she was. "Don't," she heard in an intense whisper as she reached out to do just that.

She had to stifle a scream. "You . . . are . . . awful. But thank you for not touching my shoulder." She turned to face Rafe in the darkness. His white shirt almost glowed in the moonlight.

"Yeah, you really would have been airborne then, wouldn't you?" His grin gave his shirt competition in the dim light. He drew her quietly away from the tents full of sleepers, and they settled on a low bench outside the main building from where they could still see their charges. "Thought I'd worn you out enough today so you'd sleep. What's up? Arm giving you problems?"

She shook her head then realized in this pale light he probably couldn't see her gesture. "Not exactly." *More like my heart* she felt like saying. But she didn't want to bare that much of her soul to Rafe O'Connor at this point. No matter how fond of him she was growing, she knew she wouldn't ever get that same level of sharing from him.

"Then what, exactly, is keeping you up?" She enjoyed listening to Rafe's soft, husky voice. "I can tell you exactly what's keeping me up. I keep replaying in my head variations of the conversation you and Tía Rosa probably had this afternoon. None of them sound real good."

"Why? Do you have that many secrets?"

"No, I just prefer the ones I have to stay that way, I guess. You may have noticed I'm kind of a private person."

If she weren't trying to keep quiet, Carrie would have laughed out loud. "No kidding? O'Connor, you make most hermits look extroverted. I don't understand why you're this way."

"You wouldn't. You aren't the black sheep of your family."

She tried even harder to stifle that laughter. "Wanna bet? We're all black sheep in our own way, Rafe. I cannot tell you how often I have wanted to send Laurel a thank-you note in the last six months. Marrying a law enforcement officer is the first thing she's ever done that didn't make my dad say 'Why can't you be more like your sister?' And Claire? Talk about another tough act to follow. She might as well put out the Friedens edition of *Gracious Living Magazine*."

"You're kidding? Everybody looks like one big happy family."

Carrie felt like bopping him on the head. "That's because they are, most of the time. Like every other family. Nobody's perfect, Rafe. As far as I'm concerned, that's why we've got Jesus."

"To be perfect?"

"To show us the way. Because we sure can't get it on our own. No matter how hard we try, none of us are going to be perfect in our own right."

Silence enveloped them for a while and Carrie could hear faint animal noises in the distance. There were frogs or bugs chirping and peeping differently than they did at home. And far in the distance she thought she could hear coyotes. At least she could hear what she always thought coyotes would sound like.

"Honestly, Rosa didn't tell me all that much. Although I have to admit I wish you had already told me what little she did say. You know, on paper we have a lot in common. We're both one of three kids in families of high achievers. And we both lost our moms too early."

"Any time would have been too early for me." Rafe's voice held more raw emotion than she'd heard from him. "I get along really poorly with my dad."

"Rosa mentioned that."

"I'll bet she did. But being my sweet aunt, she didn't go into details, did she?"

"Not exactly." The air between them felt charged with electricity. Carrie thought of an old trick that her sisters had taught her: chewing wintergreen candy in the dark and raising sparks. She was pretty sure Rafe could raise sparks without the candy right now, with just his words.

"I'll bet. She probably didn't say anything about the fact that we haven't spoken to each other in about six years. Rob's graduation from college and my mom's death came within a month of each other. It was like some part of her said, 'Well, they're all launched now, I can go,' and so she did. My dad didn't appreciate me pointing that out."

"Which I'm sure you did with the tact and grace you've shown in your dealings with me." Carrie leaned closer to him, trying to soften the blow of her words.

He leaned his head down on her shoulder. "Ouch. I can tell you're the youngest sibling, Carrie. You don't pull any punches at all. Here I am baring my heart to you, and you take a swipe at me."

"It's only the truth, isn't it?" Carrie's shoulder tingled where Rafe leaned his head. She held her breath, wondering what would happen next.

He rotated his head, looking up into her eyes without totally breaking contact. "Yes, it is only the truth. But it's not wrapped up in a pretty package the way I'm used to unpalatable truths being delivered. I'm a doctor. I'm used to being humored. You don't humor me, do you, Carrie?"

"Do you want me to?" Her words hung between them.

"Never. Too many other people do." He was sitting upright now, and the distance between them was closing to the point where Carrie could feel his warm breath on her cheek.

She closed her eyes, wishing she had two good hands to bury in his dark, wavy hair. One would have to do, and she reveled in the crisp, clean texture her fingers found. His mouth was insistent, seeking. Carrie's heart jumped in her chest and she saw bright light before her closed eyelids at the strength of his kiss.

The light grew brighter and Carrie let go of Rafe's neck when she realized that she was hearing sounds to go with the light. It wasn't just behind her eyelids. Looking around she saw her silent teenage tent mates playing a flashlight beam over the two of them.

"You better be heading to the bathroom." Rafe's voice was calm and soft, but quite intent. "And this better stay between the four of us come morning. Right?"

There was the faintest of giggles behind the beam of the flashlight. "Right. Sure." The light veered in the direction of the girls' dormitory, accompanied by the sounds of scuttling feet. In the faintest of whispers she could hear Heather say to Missy, "I told you so" before they disappeared. Was it Carrie's imagination or did several other tent flaps move? There was no breeze in the courtyard to ruffle the nylon or canvas.

"Still so positive the truth is a wonderful thing?" Rafe leaned his head back on the cool adobe wall of the building.

"Yes, I am." Carrie touched his lips gently with one finger. The velvet texture nearly undid her. "And I want to know more of your truths, Rafael. But not now, and not in the company of this crowd of high schoolers. Let's see if we can both go back to bed before that bunch comes back with their flashlight."

"Sounds like a plan. Maybe we can convince them they dreamed this little scene."

"Not a chance. Besides, the scene they'd dream up involving the two of us wouldn't be as innocent as one kiss in the moonlight."

"Say no more. See you in the morning, Carrie." And without any more discussion

Rafe's warm presence was gone from the bench. As the white shirt disappeared across the field of tents, Carrie found her own way back to bed. If she was extremely fortunate, she could bluff sleep before Heather and Missy got back. There was no way she was answering any questions in the dark of night.

Thursday morning Carrie woke soon after daylight as she had every morning at Casa Esperanza. Lucia sat next to her silently, waiting for her eyes to open. She was surprised that the child didn't prod or poke her. Instead, Lucia seemed to sit calmly every morning waiting for Carrie to come to her senses. Her smile lit the tent when Carrie woke up and told her good morning.

How could she leave so soon? This child had found her way into Carrie's heart in less than a week. The little girl had not had an easy life. Still, Carrie didn't think she was getting through to Lucia that she was leaving, and would be gone by the end of the day Friday. Tomorrow. It didn't seem possible.

Carrie had tried every way she knew how to communicate the facts. The Spanish phrases that she didn't know she had Rosa teach her, so that several times each day she helped Lucia count on her soft, pudgy baby fingers from one to five, just like the number of days Carrie was spending at Casa Esperanza.

It felt like the Spanish edition of *Sesame Street*, working through those basic numbers and the days of the week with the little girl. And still, even though those huge brown eyes seemed to take in everything Carrie told her, and she nodded in all the right places when Carrie asked her if she understood, she was almost positive that Lucia was not facing the truth that they had only two more days together.

She played over every scenario she could think of how not to part with Lucia on Friday night when the bus left. None of them seemed to work, in Carrie's mind.

Thursday morning she painted the indoor walls of the new dormitory and watched a crew of the older boys, supervised by Rafe and Jaime, putting in the window and door frames. All the time she hashed it over and over again in her tired brain. It didn't help that Lucia, with a floppy, well-loved rag doll, sat nearby, focused on her every move.

Carrie knew that even with all the help the Garzas could give her, the reality of a single young woman trying to adopt a child, from another country like Lucia, would be difficult, time-consuming and expensive. Difficult she could probably handle. Time-consuming would be a little more challenging, given her schedule. Expensive was the part that terrified her. Carrie had little savings and few assets.

And what on earth would she do with a child in her life as she lived it right now? She had a one-bedroom apartment and a job with unpredictable shifts. Even Fire and Rescue employees didn't make enough to allow for an expensive adoption and a preschooler's care.

Even if Lucia had no special challenges, like not understanding English or speaking any language at all, Carrie found it hard to imagine caring for an active five-year-old on a daily basis. She could probably get lots of help from her family, but the thought of what was needed was over-whelming. Plus it would probably take weeks, if not months, to get Lucia from Casa Esperanza to Friedens, Missouri.

Carrie's only alternative was not leaving on that bus tomorrow night. She knew Rafe wouldn't let her do that. Of course, she wasn't sure she herself could muster the courage to stay. She had limited money with her, and only the pitiful collection of work clothes she had brought in her duffel bag. To stay here with Lucia would mean going back home for at least a month to sort out her job, her life and her possessions just so that she could come back here.

By 10:00 a.m. Thursday morning Carrie had been working over three hours and had a pounding headache. She tried at first to blame it on paint fumes, but knew in her heart that wasn't her problem. Her headache was just an extension of the heartache she'd gained while getting so very attached to this little girl.

Rafe's hand on her shoulder nearly sent her into orbit with surprise. "Hey, take a break," he told her. "You look like you need one."

"Does it show that badly?"

"Yeah, it does. Maybe only to your personal physician, but still . . ." He shrugged the shoulders she found so very attractive. Carrie wished that those shoulders were wide enough to bear some of the burden she was carrying. But she knew that only Jesus could help her with this one. Given what he'd already told her, Rafe wasn't the man for this job.

"Okay, I'll take you up on it." Carrie put

down her paintbrush and stepped back from the wall. "Isn't this amazing?"

"Definitely. If I hadn't seen it myself before, I'd even say miraculous. Maybe it really is a miracle of sorts. I'm pretty sure we couldn't do this kind of work on our own, without God's help."

"No way. I haven't ever seen Trent or Jeremy finish cleaning their own rooms in one day. And along with the rest of this bunch they've built four rooms in less than a week."

"I know. Did you know that they're already asking when they can come back?"

"No, but it doesn't surprise me." Carrie took a deep breath, wondering if this was the opening into a conversation that she needed. "I'm trying to figure out if I, myself, want to leave."

Rafe looked puzzled. "What do you mean? We have to leave. Tomorrow night, Jake and Letty will be back with the bus, and then we're out of here."

"I know that. But you've pulled a fast one on me, O'Connor. You didn't tell me how quickly I'd fall in love down here."

He gave her a smirk. "I'm going back with the rest of them, Carrie. You don't have to worry."

She pushed his shoulder playfully. "No,

goofy. I don't mean with you. I mean with everything. Casa Esperanza. Your aunt and uncle. And especially Lucia."

"I could've seen that coming." Rafe lost any vestige of teasing he still had left. "You know that's just not possible. I haven't lost anybody yet on a mission trip. I have to take you back, Carrie. And without extra baggage, including small children, no matter how much you love them."

"Why?" Carrie sounded anguished even to herself. "Wasn't the plan to get us down here just so we would fall in love?"

"Yeah, but not that successfully. Jaime and Rosa have ways of taking care of these kids, and of placing them closer to home than Missouri."

"But they need so much. Lucia needs so much, Rafe. And she loves me. I can see it in her eyes."

Rafe put his hands on her shoulders. His deep brown eyes were even more expressive than Lucia's. "I know. I can see it there, too, Carrie. And I'm sorry about that because the last thing I expected was for you to get this involved on this trip."

"Well, I did, Rafe. What do we do about it now?" To her utter horror, Carrie burst out crying. She ran from the room, aware that everyone was staring at her, but unable to do anything.

Rafe found himself flanked by two disturbed young men. "All right," Trent said, looking grim. "What did you say to Aunt Carrie? Nobody makes her cry, man."

"It wasn't me," Rafe said. "Honest. I didn't say anything to make her cry. At least I don't think so."

"We know what happened last night outside the tents. Everybody does." Jeremy sounded accusatory.

"Oh, you do, do you? So what happened? And how did you find out?" Rafe glared at Missy, who seemed to be shrinking behind a five-gallon paint can that wasn't nearly big enough to hide her.

Jeremy backed off a little. "We heard. About you guys kissing and stuff. And I know my aunt doesn't take things like that lightly."

"Well, neither do I." It wasn't what Rafe had intended to say, but it was true. And all the kids staring at him ought to know that.

Movement near the dormitory door made his heart sink farther. Now he was really, truly in trouble. Aunt Rosa charged into the room, dragged there by Lucia. He hadn't seen the little girl leave, but she had obviously flown after Carrie and done what she thought best.

"Rafael? What is happening?" Rosa was frowning and gesturing as she spoke to him in Spanish he hoped was too fast for his teenage listeners to understand. "Lucia is frantic and in tears. Carrie is in Jaime's study, also frantic and in tears. This has to be your doing."

"For the last time, I didn't do it. She's upset about Lucia. She has the crazy idea that she can't leave here tomorrow and abandon the child."

"Maybe she can't. Maybe Lucia's link with her is what I've been praying for to make a miracle for this little one."

It was the last thing he expected to hear from his aunt. "No. That can't be right. God doesn't answer prayers that way. He answers them, sure, but not by tearing up people's lives like that just on a whim."

"Oh? You really think that?" Rosa's eyes glittered. "In your own experience, God is so predictable and practical?"

Rafe turned away from his aunt, trying to gather his wits instead of lashing out. Rosa was relentless in her attack, though. He could feel her index finger in his shoulder blade. "I still blame you for this. And you can fix it, you know."

"Can I, Tía? How? How do I fix this situation?"

Rosa looked at him with a level gaze. She took a deep breath that expanded her ample chest, and folded her arms across it. "What this little one needs even more than Carrie is a doctor. A doctor that can minister to her mind the way Jaime and I have ministered to her heart and her soul. A doctor like your father, Rafael. You can call him and then tell Carrie what you have done."

Surprise made Rafe back up several large steps away from his aunt. Could she have any idea what she was asking of him? "No. Not even for you, or this child. Or Carrie." And Rafe became the second person to leave the stunned assembly in the dormitory, not caring where he went as long as it was away.

Chapter Eleven

Jaime Garza didn't seem to know what to do with a crying woman. He appeared even more uncomfortable than Rafe, which was saying a lot. Carrie tried to compose herself so that they could talk sensibly.

He had handed her one of his faded bandanna kerchiefs to wipe her face. "I'm sorry," she said, trying not to sniffle or hiccup. "I don't usually get this way. Not at all. I'm the tough one on Fire and Rescue. They say I can do anything."

"But this time you could not. And it makes you very frustrated."

"Yes. I want to do everything I can for Lucia, Pastor Garza. But I'm leaving tomorrow and she can't come with me. And Rafe is no help at all. He even said he was sorry he took me down here."

Pastor Garza looked startled. "That is what he said?"

"Not exactly. But he did say he was sorry I was so distressed over Lucia, because he couldn't do anything about it."

"And he cannot. At least he thinks he cannot." Carrie tried to figure out what it was that Jaime meant. "Through the window just now, I saw Lucia come after you and get Rosa. They went back to the dormitory. Then Rafael ran quickly out the door, in the direction of the dirt road behind the buildings. He and his aunt have had words, it seems."

"Oh, boy. I bet the kids are really upset now." Carrie pushed herself out of the chair. "I better go back there and ride herd over everybody."

"I think Rosa can do that. Perhaps I will go help her. Maybe you can go ride herd, as you put it, on Rafael instead."

It was the last thing Carrie wanted to do. In her heart, she knew Jaime was right. Nothing good would come from storming away from Rafe and bursting into tears. Lucia wouldn't be helped by it, and neither would she. "All right. Give me a minute to put myself together."

Jaime looked as if he wanted to tell her something else, something important. But he stayed silent a moment as if in thought. Once he spoke, Carrie could tell he'd decided against saying whatever he intended earlier.

"There is cool water in that basin." Jaime pointed to the corner of his study. "I keep some there to refresh myself in the middle of these hot afternoons when I must go tutor the older children in mathematics. Wash your face and go after Rafael. I will go talk to your young friends."

"Thank you." Carrie was glad there wasn't a mirror in the corner by Jaime's cool water. She was sure all she'd see would be her own red eyes and blotchy face. Her throat was scratchy and she felt sweaty and out of sorts. Her cast was itchier than usual.

She prayed as she put herself in some semblance of order. It wasn't a very organized prayer. But it was fervent and heartfelt. She wanted so much right now — for Lucia, for herself and even for Rafe. Was any of it God's will?

Sighing audibly, Carrie tried to put all of her troubles in God's hands. This time it was even harder than usual. She dunked the bandanna in the water and wrung it out as well as she could with one hand. It was awkward and slow. The cool water felt good on her face. After a few passes over her cheeks she stopped glowing like a stoplight.

In a moment or two she was ready to go

find Rafe. She still had no idea what she would say to him once she found him, but it was time to find out.

Most of the country in back of his aunt and uncle's property was desert, and Rafe stared out into the horizon. The only breaks in the landscape were scrubby cactus and even scrubbier trees. What had he done back there? What was he supposed to do? He blinked in the harsh light, and looked down at his own hands.

They weren't very impressive hands when he stopped to stare at them. They couldn't do half of what he wanted them to, even after all the years of medical training. Perhaps no human hands could. He wanted to give back the best of what he was to God. Surely that was what God wanted, wasn't it?

Rafe had a feeling that Carrie wasn't as selective as he was. She seemed better at giving her all to God to use as He would. Perhaps that was what aggravated him the most about her. Carrie could open her heart to God, and to little children like Lucia while he couldn't do that.

He was so deep into his thoughts and prayers that he never heard Carrie coming. When she stood behind him and called his name, he nearly jumped off the rock he was sitting on.

"Sorry," she said, putting a slim hand on his shoulder. "I didn't mean to scare you to death."

"Hey, I'm not usually on the receiving end of that kind of feeling. No problem."

"We've got a few problems here, Rafael. I'm sorry I added to them by flying out of there like I did."

"I deserved it, Carrie." He was standing now, and took her hands. "Tía Rosa reminded me just how much I deserved it."

"Your uncle looked out the window and said you two had had words. I suspect that was the understatement of the week. Your aunt doesn't strike me as the type to stay silent long."

"She isn't. I think it's a family thing." Rafe marveled in how right it felt to stand here, holding Carrie's hands and just talking. Even having to work one of his hands around the outcropping of her cast felt good. "My mom tended to fly off the handle once in a while, too, especially with me. Usually it was for the best of reasons. Looking back on things, I almost wish she'd done it more."

"Really?" Carrie looked puzzled. "You

wish your mom had yelled at you more?"

"Yelled at somebody, at least. Maybe she wouldn't have bottled up her frustrations, or whatever led to her dying so young. The newer research I've seen on heart disease and anger management seems to take a real Biblical attitude."

"Wow. I'm on the forefront of medical knowledge without even knowing it." Carrie's grin was impish. "Just for apologizing for making a fool of myself."

"Not a fool. You are right to care so much about Lucia. She's a sweet little girl and she cares about you, too. That much I can see, Carrie."

"When I was in his office, Jaime said something I didn't understand. I told him you couldn't help me with my problems with Lucia, and he said that you only *think* you can't. What's he talking about?"

Rafe realized he was going to have to tell her everything. Then the light in her eyes, which shone for him with such a hopeful gleam, would go out permanently. Of course that was only what he deserved. But Rafe hated to lose that glow. It had felt so good.

"He's talking about the same thing that Rosa called me to task on just now. I told you my father was a doctor. And that we haven't spoken in years."

"Right. And while I don't agree with your reasoning there, I know we can't make you do anything, Rafe. Every family has its rough spots, but the family members have to take care of them themselves."

"True. However, what I haven't told you is that my dad's not just any doctor. Russell O'Connor is probably one of the better-known psychiatrists in San Diego. And he specializes in treating children."

Understanding dawned on Carrie's face. Any moment now she would probably let go of his hands and walk away. Rafe was surprised when it didn't happen. "So your father might be able to help Lucia? I expect after being married to someone from Mexico all those years, he speaks Spanish well."

"Excellently. The conversation in my house, growing up, flowed back and forth from one language to the other without anybody ever thinking about it. When I was in grade school I used to get in trouble at school for unconsciously starting a sentence in one language and finishing in another."

Carrie's brow wrinkled. "So what you're telling me is that your father would be the perfect person to help Lucia. Then why won't Rosa and Jaime just call him?"

"Out of respect to me, while I'm here. They know how poorly we've gotten along, and while they don't agree with it, either, they feel it's my job to bridge the gap. Besides, I'm not sure my dad would talk to either of them unless I talked to him first. I might have said some pretty rash things at some point about the Garzas being my substitute family."

Now she had let go of his hands, but Carrie didn't walk away from him. "Wow. This is a heavy situation, isn't it, Rafe?"

"The heaviest."

Carrie was still standing close enough to touch him, and hadn't moved away. "You didn't have to tell me all this. You could have let me go on thinking there was nothing you could do to help Lucia."

"I could have. But I demand the truth from other people, and expect to tell it myself. Especially to those I . . . care about." He couldn't bring himself to say he loved her. He wasn't even sure if it was true yet. Even if it were the truth, Rafe wasn't sure if he could say something like that to Carrie. Bad things seemed to happen to people he loved. She didn't need to be included in that.

"I appreciate the honesty." Carrie swallowed so hard, Rafe could see the motion of her throat. It made her look terribly vulnerable. "It's a difficult thing to ask of you, though, isn't it? Sharing that kind of truth with me, and wrestling with what to do about it."

"The hardest. I still don't know if I can do the right thing and call him. Not even for you or Lucia." He felt like the world's biggest heel telling her that, but now was not the time to back down on honesty.

Carrie's blue eyes sparkled. "Do you want me to keep praying for you along with my prayers for Lucia? We've got thirty-some hours left here. Surely this can resolve itself in that amount of time."

"I'm glad you think so." Now it was Rafe who felt like walking away. He didn't deserve this kind of consideration from Carrie. Didn't know what to do with it now that he'd gotten it. Her acceptance where he'd expected anger put him off balance.

"I have to think so. It's just the kind of person I am. My dad says people either expect the best or the worst out of every situation. I guess I'm one of those people that expect the best. Maybe that isn't the most logical thing, but it's the way I'm made."

Something about the way she said that made Rafe smile in spite of himself. "I have to tell you, away from all those kids, I like the way you're made, Carrie. And I mean that in every sense of the word. But they better not hear me say that."

"Got found out, did we? I didn't think Missy and Heather could keep quiet." Carrie was smiling a little now, too.

"Yeah. You better go back in there with a smile on your face and try to tell them everything is all right. I got a real talking-to from Jeremy and Trent for making you cry."

She stuck out her chin. "You didn't make me cry, O'Connor. Not all by yourself."

"Tell them that, will you? I'm not exactly the man of the hour right now."

Carrie sighed. "Guess I'll go set them straight. You coming back with me?"

Rafe shook his head. "Not quite yet. I have some more heavy thinking to do, and this is kind of a thinking rock."

"Is it a praying rock, too? Because you sound like that's the only thing that will totally solve your problem."

"I'll make sure it's a praying rock, too, Carrie. You can count on it." She hugged him silently and headed back to the buildings. Rafe watched her go, and as he watched her, he began a halting prayer. It was a start.

Carrie was never sure what Jaime had told the kids, but they asked few questions when she came back. Trent, Jeremy and Ashleigh gathered around her looking for reassurance. Ashleigh was dotted with white paint, and nearly overwhelmed by Lucia riding high on one hip. "She must know we're related, because while you were gone she wouldn't let go of me," she told Carrie.

However the moment that Carrie was back in front of her, Lucia reached for Carrie. A contented sigh escaped her when she was in Carrie's arms, and she cuddled like a much younger child. Her action sent a stab of pain through Carrie again. How were they going to resolve all this? Surely God had a plan for them all, one He'd reveal to her before they were ready to leave tomorrow night.

"Thanks, Ash," she told her niece. "Isn't she the sweetest little girl you've ever seen?"

"She really is. I bet she's almost as sweet as my new *sister* will be," she said in a tone that hinted at her wish to aggravate Jeremy.

Carrie couldn't help smiling at that, which made Lucia even more content. The little girl's soft hand reached up and patted her shoulder and Carrie found herself instinctively rocking the child on her hip.

It was a marvel what could happen if you let it, she told herself. How God could use bodies and hearts and minds to His purpose if you just got out of His way. Maybe that was what she needed to do in this situation. Maybe she needed to get out of God's way and let Him do the work here. She prayed to be able to do just that as she walked around the inside of the dormitory, inspecting all the work that had been done in her absence.

Lucia was asleep in her arms after one circuit of the building. Her hair was damp in the heat of the day and she was a heavy weight on Carrie's hip. Still, there was a sweetness about feeling the little girl resting on her chest that made Carrie feel right about everything.

Even the bathrooms in the boys' and girls' dormitory rooms were taking shape nicely. These bathrooms they were building were more complex than what was in the old dormitories where they'd spent that first night. With help from local men who seemed to know about plumbing and simple electricity, the rooms they were building had more complicated modern facilities, as well as a mirror over each bathroom sink.

Carrie watched as teams of youth group members and local people set light switches along each wall. A team of girls worked in the girls' bathroom, making sure the polished metal mirrors were attached to the wall right. Passing the bank of mirrors, Carrie looked into them. She knew she was a sight by now, but what she saw amazed her.

Yes, she was rumpled and brown from laboring in the sun. She was still casually dressed in shorts and a cotton shirt. But the sleeping figure of Lucia balanced on her hip made the whole picture complete somehow. Even though they looked nothing alike, with Lucia's dark hair and skin, and Carrie's freckles still standing out in relief across her cheeks, they looked right together. The beauty of the picture they made nearly took Carrie's breath away.

This has to be what you have in mind for us, she said silently to God. *I have no idea how to make this picture reality. But show me how, Lord. Show me how.* And then from the other side of the room someone was calling for help with a fastener, and Lucia shifted in her sleep. Life went on no matter whether she wanted it to or not. Carrie murmured softly to the girl calling her, walking as quickly as she could with her sweet, heavy burden.

As she walked past the doorway to the outside, she caught a glimpse of a figure in the distance. Rafe was still sitting on his rock, thinking or praying. Maybe he was doing both. She shifted Lucia, feeling sweat in the small of her back from the effort of carrying the sleeping child. It was time to put her to bed.

Letting one of the youth group kids nearest the door know where she was going, Carrie crossed to the main building and through to Lucia's dormitory room. She settled her down on the bunk, hoping she would stay asleep. The child stirred, but didn't wake. Carrie watched her lips moving silently. She seemed to be forming words. She could only wonder what she was saying, and if she would ever say it out loud.

Carrie patted the child's shoulder for a moment, settling her deeper into sleep. Once she was reassured that she wasn't going to wake up right away, she headed to the kitchen to tell Rosa what was going on.

She'd get a quick drink of water and go back to work on the dormitory. It would keep her mind occupied with things she could actually do something about, instead of that complex man out there sitting on a rock.

Working kept her mind occupied most of the afternoon. At some point Rafe had come in and joined the work crew. She could hear him in the other dormitory room, supervising operations from time to time.

Lucia bounded back into the new girls' dormitory late in the afternoon, eyes bright and darting around until she found Carrie. She was content sitting near her again, not needing to be held. She had paper and three crayons with her, and was happy sitting against one of the walls drawing a picture. She looked up frequently to make sure Carrie wasn't out of sight. Just knowing she was nearby was enough.

The building made incredible strides through the long, hot day. What had started out as a rough area in the morning looked almost like a home by the time Rosa came to call everyone to dinner. "You are marvels, all of you," she chorused, patting the youth group kids on the back and giving them lots of praise. "Now come in and eat. You must be starved."

After all the work and turmoil of the day, Carrie looked forward to a meal and some rest. She washed up with the rest of the workers, trying to keep order among those inclined to water fights. Jaime said an even more eloquent blessing than usual, and everybody dove into dinner.

She still hadn't said anything to Rafe since their glances met over the table. They had both echoed Jaime's "Amen" to grace, and gone about eating. Carrie was using every ounce of willpower she still had left not to ask him if he'd come to a decision.

Only after the older children had cleared the table and brought out cookies for dessert, with coffee for the grown-ups and more milk for the children, did Carrie notice that Rafe was looking at her intently. She looked back, trying to read words in the warmth of those dark eyes. It was no use. Even after getting to know him better, Rafe O'Connor's eyes still didn't provide a window into his innermost thoughts.

"How's it going?" she asked him softly, breaking off a piece of her cookie and popping it into Lucia's mouth.

"Rough. I feel like I've wrestled with my

thoughts so long that I'm as sore as if I'd wrestled with bears." His face looked somber, close to anguish. "Forgive me, Carrie, but I just can't do it. Not today, anyhow."

"Then there has to be another answer. You'll see, Rafe." Carrie was surprised at her own optimism. But she'd told Rafe earlier that she believed the best, and it was true. She didn't know yet how God would provide it, but at some point in the next twenty-four hours she was sure she would find out.

Chapter Twelve

Friday's wake-up call nearly did Carrie in. She didn't feel like she'd slept that well the night before. Even though she'd taken apart her sleeping bag and ground cover before bed, and made sure there were no large stones under her bed, she still tossed and turned. Missy and Heather swore they hadn't let Lucia into the tent, but she was still there in the early light, sitting next to Carrie's shoulder.

"What am I going to do with you, little one?" Carrie stroked the little girl's smooth cheek. It felt soft and incredibly tender, like the skin of a ripe peach.

Lucia smiled that high-wattage smile, leaning into Carrie's touch. How would Carrie deal with life tomorrow without her? She couldn't come up with any solution. The best thing she could hope for was that somehow she could convince Rafe to get his father involved with Casa Esperanza, giving them a closer source of good health care, both physical and mental, for the children.

She'd still worry about Lucia and all the others if that happened. But at least she'd know that they were being well taken care of. Jaime and Rosa were doing all they could. And their care had made an incredible difference in the lives of these children.

But deep in her heart Carrie felt that she had been brought here for one specific purpose. The youth group would have gotten along just as well if someone else had been their chaperon. Even after four days, she felt that she was here to make a difference for Lucia. Getting on the bus tonight and driving away didn't feel like she'd made enough difference. Even if she came back here in a month or two, when she could arrange it, ready to adopt Lucia and take her home to Friedens, there would still be more damage to the fragile child.

How many partings had this baby-faced little girl already endured? She'd lost her father before she knew she had one, and her mother, when she was a tiny child. Carrie had no way of knowing how many different situations Lucia and her mother had been in before the mother's arrest that led to their final parting.

Life at Casa Esperanza was the most stable thing Lucia had ever known, though there was still plenty of change. Children came and went, and there were more than seventy of them who needed attention from Jaime, Rosa and the limited staff. Life was crowded and hectic at best, even though it was full of as much love as the Garzas could give these kids.

Now for reasons known only to God, Lucia had latched on to Carrie like a life-line. And she was preparing to leave. She had never planned to stay more than this one week, and she hadn't dreamed that she'd get so attached to any of these children. Still, it had happened and now she had to deal with it as best she could.

Carrie felt prayed out. She'd taken this in near-constant prayer to the Lord every time she sat down and rested, or in those long hours of the night she was counting rocks under her sleeping bag. There just weren't any clear answers. None that she could do anything about, anyway. Everything still seemed to come back to Rafe and his dad.

She knew she'd wrestle with it all morning, too, and during devotions with the kids after breakfast. It was time to face the fact that it was time to get up and moving. Not that Lucia was going to let her do anything else. She'd gotten tired of waiting patiently for Carrie to get up. On her knees beside the sleeping bag, she was rooting around through Carrie's duffel bag. Heather and Missy were laughing, watching her ferret out Carrie's clothing.

"Oh, no, I'm doing that myself," Carrie told her, lifting the child out of her duffel bag. "You can sit here and watch me, or help with buttons or something, but you're not picking out my outfit."

Carrie found the least objectionable clothing she could, even managing to come up with a clean shirt that hadn't seen the light of day. It was a bright cotton shirt with a small flower pattern. Lucia approved.

Once they'd gone together to the bathroom off the girls' dormitory, and Lucia had followed Carrie through all the steps of her morning rituals that Carrie would let her follow, she looked around to see that nobody was watching them. Bending down, she popped the cap off her tube of nearly colorless lip gloss. "Now this is just between you and me," she told Lucia, then put a swipe on those baby lips. The smile she got in return was brighter than anything yet. She boosted herself up on top of the sink, looking in the slightly dull metal mirror and making a kissing motion.

Carrie could see her, for an instant, doing this same thing at ten or twelve. Watching Lucia, she knew without a doubt now that she wanted to be there to see her. "Show me how, Lord. Show me the way." Her prayer was almost silent, just breathed into the nearly empty room. Lucia, deeply intent on her introduction to cosmetics, didn't even turn around in response. In the waiting silence, Carrie could feel a murmur like a rush of wings. She hoped it was God's response.

Today's activity in the new dorms was purposeful and loud. The walls and roof and windows were in place. The fixtures had been installed in the bathrooms and there were lights attached to the ceiling beams and electrical conduit running up the walls. It wasn't nearly as posh as any of the youth group was used to for everyday living, but it would make a tremendous difference in the lives of these kids.

Jaime and Rosa were directing crews moving in furniture and hanging indoor shutters on the wide windows. In the older dormitories, other youth group kids were taking apart bunk beds to make single beds for everyone. Chests and desks were marked move or stay, depending on their owners.

Carrie stood in the middle of one of the new rooms, trying to realize that before they came here, this had been a bare concrete slab. A few weeks before that it had been nothing but dirt. Now it was a dormitory that would house up to twenty-five kids comfortably, and up to fifty in crowded conditions.

"Think we did okay?" Rafe nearly made her jump, sneaking up behind her while she was so deep in thought.

"You know we did. There's still more to do . . ." She trailed off. She couldn't ask him again about getting a doctor for the kids. That would be too much. And Carrie had to admit that although the Lord had laid this concern on her heart, He might not have laid it equally on Rafe.

"Plenty, but maybe it's not our job, Carrie." He walked around her and straightened a bed frame. "There will be others following behind us. There always are. And I don't know about you, but I have plenty to do at home."

Carrie turned to face him. "How can you do that? Just go back each time and pick up your normal life, knowing that all these kids are here, and what their lives are like?"

He looked at her with a level gaze, then crossed the distance between them, putting a hand on each of her shoulders. "I can't. A big chunk of my heart stays here, which is why I use all of my vacation every year to do things like this. I've been coming here to work since I was twelve, Carrie. There wasn't any Casa Esperanza then, just a dream that Rosa and Jaime had, and one my mother wanted to help them realize."

She felt a pang of guilt as she thought about the number of hours Rafe had put in here. "Guess I really look like the new kid on the block, giving you a hard time." His warm brown eyes flashed with emotion and Carrie could feel his hands gripping her shoulders even more firmly.

"No, I'm glad you've gotten this involved here, this quickly. It means it will be even easier to get you back here again."

Carrie brought her own hands up on his shoulders, holding on to him for strength. "It's worse than that. I think you may have to leave me here."

He let go of her. "You know I can't do that."

"What if I didn't give you a choice? I am

an adult, you know."

"All too well. But think of the situation that would put me in, Carrie. First of all, I'd have no other help but Jake and Letty on the bus ride back. And second, how do you expect me to explain to your family that I took you to Mexico and let you stay there?"

"I'd call them before you got back to Friedens. I wouldn't put you in that position."

Rafe's smile held more than a touch of relief. "That's good to know. But it's still out of the question. I need you, Carrie. I need you on that bus and helping me out on the way back. Promise me you'll go home with us tonight no matter what."

She took a deep breath, wanting to do what he asked, but knowing in her heart she couldn't. "I'd like to promise that. But I don't break promises, especially to people I care about, Rafe. And there's no way I'll make the one you're asking me to. It would be much too easy to break."

"You'd do more good for her if you went home, you know." Rafe's gaze went to the corner of the room where Lucia sat, playing with her rag doll. "She's got a good stable home here, a roof over her head, food and clothing. She knows the love of

Jesus and of other people. You could make sure she keeps getting all of that simply by sending Jaime and Rosa money for her."

"But I couldn't hug her that way. And she wouldn't be sitting next to my bed waiting for me to wake up every morning."

Rafe sighed. "That's true. But, Carrie, I have to be blunt. Casa Esperanza is a shoestring operation. You've seen that. It can't support one more person. In order to stay, you'd have to get a job somewhere near here, fast. And that isn't going to happen when you have no work visa for this country, no contacts across the border in San Diego and a cast on one arm. So you're going to have to go home, like it or not."

"That's a definite not." It was all Carrie could do not to burst into tears of frustration for the second time in two days. "Why do you have to be so rational and logical, O'Connor?"

"Somebody has to be. You're letting your heart and your impulses rule again and we've seen where that has gotten you before." He tapped lightly on her cast.

"It got me to follow you here in the first place. And up until right now, I would have said it was getting me in even deeper trouble, because I think I was actually falling in love with you."

"Was?" Rafe challenged.

"Was. Anybody who can look at little children and be this detached in the face of their pain isn't the man I want to love." And again, just like yesterday, Carrie nearly flew out of the dormitory. At least this time she kept some of her dignity. Thanks to that, she didn't create such a stir as she left.

Today she didn't head toward the kitchen to find Rosa. There wasn't anything Rafe's aunt could do about her feelings this time. This was for her to work out by herself.

She sat down on one of the benches on the deep porch. It was the coolest place at Casa Esperanza.

"This isn't working out well," she said out loud, needing a vent for the frustration she felt with God, with herself and with Rafael O'Connor. "If you're showing me that this is the way to solve all my problems, Lord, I feel lost. Like I've taken a wrong turn on the path somewhere."

As if in answer, Lucia was there beside her. It was only then that Carrie realized she was crying again. She'd cried more in the last two days than she had in at least two years. Maybe being around Rafe wasn't so good for her.

Lucia scrambled up on the bench next to her, but that wasn't enough to satisfy the child. She boosted herself up on Carrie's lap. When she plopped herself firmly and settled in, she patted Carrie's cheek with one warm hand. Since they'd both been moving furniture and playing in the dormitory, Carrie was sure her cheek was now smudged with baby handprints. It made it all the harder to keep from sobbing out loud.

Lucia didn't move her hand away, nor did she break her gaze with Carrie. Those deep brown eyes, even more expressive than Rafe's, bored into her. With stubborn silence, Lucia seemed to be trying to tell her something. In case Carrie didn't get her drift, Lucia now put the other soft, grubby little hand on her other cheek.

And then it happened. A rough, husky sound, not much more than a whisper, grated out of the little girl's throat. "Mami?"

Carrie tried to suppress a gasp. Lucia was talking. She didn't even have to translate to know what she meant. "Mommy" was much the same in any language. "What, baby? I'm here."

"Mami. No irse. No irse." Mommy, don't go

away. Don't go away. Her words couldn't have been clearer if Lucia had screamed them.

"Oh, baby, I won't." Carrie leaned back against the bench, feeling overwhelmed by the power of what she had just heard. "I can't. And Rafe is going to be so mad at me." Because in one brief instant Carrie knew just what she had to do and how she had to do it. And Rafe wasn't going to like it one bit.

Lunch was chaotic, to say the least. All the older children who could get their teachers to let them out of Friday afternoon classes had done so. Everybody was coming back for the dedication ceremony for the new building. All the youth group kids were in a state of giddy exhaustion that made them more obnoxious than usual.

In all the confusion, Rafe didn't think much about the fact that he hadn't seen Carrie. After their tangle this morning he truly didn't expect her to sit next to him at lunch and be friendly. That would have been too much, even for Carrie.

The crowd that gathered to meet Jake and Letty when the coach pulled in next to the building was raucous. Letty made great exclamations over the building, letting four of the girls from Casa Esperanza lead her through the new wing. Jake was a little quieter in his praise, but it meant just as much to the horde of little boys who escorted him through their new space.

Neither Carrie nor Lucia put in an appearance for the tour, and Rafe began to get concerned. He could understand Carrie wanting a last private lunch with the little girl. But where were they for the afternoon's excitement?

Soon there were only four tents left standing in their courtyard enclosure, and he still hadn't seen Carrie during the packing up. He began to worry. The kids were doing a great job all by themselves of taking down the tents and getting their belongings stowed back in the duffels. He deputized Trent and Ashleigh to keep the peace and went into the main building to talk to Rosa.

"All right, something is up. And I want to know right now. Where's Carrie? Why haven't I seen her or Lucia since before lunch?"

The last thing he expected from his aunt was for her to start crying.

"They're all right, aren't they? She didn't run away, did she?" His heart jumped out of his chest in a kind of panic that didn't even happen during the worst moments in the emergency room.

"Nothing like that. I don't know how to tell you what has happened." Rosa sat down on a stool in the kitchen and folded her hands in her lap. "You are not a believer in miracles, Rafael. Not the kind that does not include bricks and mortar. But your Carrie is such a believer, and today she and I saw one."

"I have no idea what you're talking about."

"Lucia spoke. I heard her myself. Your Carrie said she asked God for a sign and He provided it."

"First of all, she isn't 'my' Carrie."

"Isn't she? Are you so sure about that?" His aunt rose from her seat, and the normal fire he expected was back in her eyes.

"Pretty sure. After today, almost positive. I thought we were getting someplace, but not after everything that happened today. You're right about my not believing in miracles. Not the kind you're talking about."

"She spoke. I heard her. Carrie says she did, more than once. Rafael, the child called her *Mami*."

"And that's supposed to make me drop all my preconceived notions and say it's just great that the woman who is supposed to be helping me get twenty kids back to Missouri tonight went to San Diego on a wild-goose chase instead."

It was easy to see from his aunt's expression that he'd hit pay dirt. "That's what she did, isn't it? She went up there to take the girl to my father, didn't she? How'd she get to town to the trolley stop? Did you take her?"

"Ramon." It was the name of one of the local young men, who served as Jaime's handyman when he was available. "They used the truck."

"And I'm sure everything was legal and aboveboard to spirit a five-year-old orphan across the border for a medical appointment nobody even made for her." Rosa clammed up and waved away his concerns. That alone told him that however they got Lucia over the border, it might not have been exactly on the up-and-up.

"They will be back in a few hours. All will be well. You'll see." His aunt's look dared him to argue.

This was one impulsive decision too many from Carrie. Rafe felt anger flaring in him in a way he hadn't in years. "Yeah, well, whether she's back or not, that bus is leaving after dinner."

Chapter Thirteen

Usually dedication ceremonies were Rafe's favorite part of the whole process when he built something at Casa Esperanza. This time, it wasn't nearly as much fun without Carrie there. He was so distracted by his anger over what she and Rosa had done that he could hardly concentrate on Jaime's words or the children's music.

The youth group held off from openly rebelling, but that was the best he could say about their attitude. When he came back from talking with Rosa, he called everybody together and sat down for a difficult discussion.

It had interrupted several games and attacks of high spirits to get them sitting down in the first place. When he told them that Carrie had run off on them to take Lucia across the border, he didn't expect the responses he got. There was a lot of praising the Lord and exclamation over Lucia regaining her speech, and no surprise or condemnation over Carrie's rash decision.

But then they were kids. What had he really expected? He tried to explain to them, as simply as possible, why this was such a lousy idea on Carrie's part. And why he was not delaying their departure past the eight o'clock deadline he'd already set for them.

They'd stared at him in what looked like stunned silence. "You're kidding, right?" Ashleigh finally asked.

"Not a bit. Remember, before we left Missouri we all signed a contract that said we'd abide by the rules the group set up. Your parents signed those contracts along with you, and it included not going off anyplace without permission from the adults in charge. Failure to obey the contract would have meant that you would have been sent home at your own expense as a consequence of your behavior. I don't see why it should be any different for Carrie."

Several of the girls looked to be near tears, but they didn't say anything else. Trent and Jeremy talked quietly to each other, but they didn't come up and talk to him. It was a subdued group that participated in the dedication. Every sound from the road in front of the buildings made heads turn. But the few vehicles that went past were only farm trucks or battered cars.

Tía Rosa tried to inject as much fiesta atmosphere into their last meal together as she could. Things had already been prepared for a big dinner, and the tables were decorated with candles and bright paper flowers. For the sake of the children, Rafe wanted his youth group kids to get into the spirit of the party as much as possible.

His aunt tried to talk to him during the course of the meal, but he pushed off her attempts. "You are making a big mistake. One that you can't undo, Rafael." Her expression was as stern as he'd ever seen it. "If you do this thing the way you threaten to, you will wound a gentle spirit. I think you will wound her past repair."

"That's her choice, Tía. Nobody told her to go off to San Diego and go against everything I asked her to do. I even asked her to promise me earlier that she wouldn't do anything crazy like this, but she refused."

"Why are you so angry with her? Because she's doing what you can't?"

"She's doing what I told her not to. And

she's doing foolish things. That is why I'm so angry."

"It wouldn't be because you are afraid of her impulsive actions? Afraid that if you stay here, your father will come back with her and you still don't know what to say to him?"

His first impulse was to deny the truth of that statement, but Rafe knew he couldn't. If he was going to fault Carrie for her lack of honesty, he couldn't go that direction himself. "Maybe that's part of it. I guess I am pretty comfortable with the life I've made for myself that doesn't include him. But it's not just that. Carrie and I have tangled before about her making rash decisions."

Jaime came and joined Tía Rosa. "Rafael, I cannot stay silent any longer. I have heard what you are saying. Neither you or Carrie is totally right here. When Rosa told me what they were planning, I knew you would be unhappy. I was not altogether pleased myself. But could you at least consider that this may be what God has led Carrie to do?"

That pushed him over the edge. "Not for a minute. Carrie Collins doesn't ever sit still long enough to let God lead her into anything. She just rushes off in the first direction she thinks is right, with no consideration for anybody else."

"No consideration for anybody else, or no consideration for you? Isn't this what we're talking about here?" Rosa crossed her arms over her ample chest. "You are hurt because this lovely young woman does not do what you tell her. You are also hurt because she can let go of all your rules and laws and say yes to God's calling even before you hear the same call."

"This is ridiculous." Rafe was closer to losing his temper than he had been in years. His fists were clenched and every muscle in his body felt tight with tension. "You make it sound like Carrie's the one doing the right thing here. I'm only sticking to what we agreed on. What we planned to do in the first place."

Jaime looked at him as if trying to form exactly the right thought. From the look in his eyes, Rafe could tell he wasn't going to like what his uncle had to say. "Sometimes, Rafael, God is not all plans. There is law, but there is also Gospel. Which do you think Jesus would have you follow today, in this situation?"

Rafe couldn't answer that one. He knew what Jaime wanted him to say, but it felt like too easy an answer. Too flippant to be true and much too frightening to consider. "I have to be by myself for a while."

"Good. We still have dessert for the children. Maybe that will give you enough time to come to the right decision." Rosa let him go, and from the corner of his eye Rafe could see her getting her helpers in line to serve the sweets. Even his aunt knew the value of rules and routine, as she smoothly ran Casa Esperanza. Why was she so argumentative tonight?

He had to admit he'd been prickly himself. Weren't his reasons the best ones? He argued them to himself all the way out of the building and toward the same rock he'd occupied earlier in the week.

Sitting on his rock perch wasn't very comfortable tonight. The rock cooled down quickly once it got dark. So there he sat, on an uncomfortable spot that was fast becoming almost unbearable. Through open doorways he could hear the kids eating and laughing.

He felt like an idiot sitting out here. Any decision he made would be wrong. If he pushed to go ahead and do what he felt was right, everybody else would be mad at him. If he waited for Carrie, she would win this battle of wills they had been playing since the day they met. And to top things off, he would come face-to-face with his father for the first time in years. They'd been estranged for so long now that he had no idea what to say when they met again.

"Why did you have to go and do this?" Rafe said aloud. He knew Carrie couldn't hear him. But since she wasn't there to argue with in person, talking to thin air while sitting on a rock would have to do. Nobody in the world got under his skin like this woman did. If he had anything to say about it, nobody else ever would, either.

The stars were starting to come out and Rafe still had no answers to his questions. The rock was too uncomfortable to sit on by now, so he got down and started toward the doorway. The first person he encountered was Jake.

The older man in his battered cowboy hat stopped him a few feet into the room. "So, should I unload that bus? Are you ready to hunker down and wait for that girl?"

Just the fact that everyone seemed to expect him to do just that told Rafe he finally had his answer. "No, I'm not going to wait for her. She knows when we're leaving. And we're going to leave."

Jake scowled. "You're going to have to

drive the first leg of the trip yourself then. Because I'm not going to be the one responsible for leaving that sweet little girl here."

That sweet little girl? "Fine. I'll get everybody ready to go. Fifteen minutes and we're out of here." Rafe surprised himself by being able to keep his voice level and not shout. He was in charge here. What kind of leader would he be if he let Carrie get away with this stunt? He'd never be able to keep order in the youth group again.

He went to the front of the room and stood next to Jaime. The kids quieted down. "You've got fifteen minutes. Do what you need to in order to leave. Say your goodbyes and Pastor Garza will ride with us as far as the end of their road and pray us on our way."

"I will. But I still don't think you're making the right decision." Jaime's words were soft enough that only Rafael could hear.

"This time I have to disagree. It's the best thing for me to do and I'm sure of it."

Jaime shrugged and turned to his wife. She looked upset, but didn't say anything. Rafe got a flash of memory from years before of his mother's expression when he,

Renata or Rob used to disappoint her. Seeing that same look on Rosa's face made him want to change his mind for a moment. But he couldn't; he'd gone too far now to back down.

The room was a stir of kids of various ages. The teens had all gotten attached to one child or another from Casa Esperanza, and these last partings were hard. That was one of the reasons Rafe was so determined to stay on schedule. It wouldn't get any easier by putting them off.

His own things were gathered for leaving, and he hugged his aunt goodbye. She didn't say much, but then neither did he. Jake and Letty were having a discussion in the corner, which ended with Letty giving Rafe a look much more pointed than those his aunt had been giving him.

The kids seemed to take as long as they dared to get on the bus and get settled. Jaime boarded with them, and Rafe closed the doors and started the engine. The headlights were welcome on the dark, narrow road leading away from Casa Esperanza. Leaving was never his favorite part of these trips, and tonight's departure was probably the worst one yet. Because now he also had to struggle with his decision.

Still feel like you're doing the right thing? a voice in his head whispered. He ignored it and put the bus into gear. They lurched forward and it took a moment to get his bearings on the rutted road. Negotiating this stretch of road in the dark wasn't easy.

When he could see the gates up ahead, Rafe began to congratulate himself. They were going to get to where they needed to go, then pull off and let Jaime say his farewell blessing. Once they got through the gates they'd be on their way and nothing was going to stop them.

A bigger rut than usual nearly wrenched the wheel out of his hand. There was a bang, followed by noises he couldn't describe, but recognized all too well. The bus slowly lurched to a near halt. "Nice going. I don't know what you managed to run over, but we've got a flat." Jake sounded almost happy about it.

"So we'll fix it." Rafe's teeth were clenched.

"Not quickly we won't. This isn't like fixing a flat tire on some little bitty car. First this coach has to be unloaded." Jake turned to Jaime, who was looking out the front window of the coach. Rafe could tell his uncle was trying very hard not to laugh. "Know anybody with the kind of equipment I'll need to jack this thing up?"

"Perhaps. But on a Friday night after dark, like this, it won't be easy to find them and get them out here."

"Well, that's the breaks." Jake was definitely smiling now.

Rafe grabbed the microphone. "Okay. Let's all get off the bus and start unloading. The quicker we get this done, the quicker we'll be on the road again." Nobody argued with Rafe, and they all complied after a fashion. True, nobody bounded to the front of the coach and hopped down the steps quickly. But in a matter of minutes they were all outside, and Jake unlocked the luggage compartments.

"Both sides? You've got to unload both sides?" Rafe was near shouting now.

"Sure." Jake and Jaime were both stifling grins now. "Can't do it any other way."

If he didn't know better, Rafe would have said he had a conspiracy on his hands. But he'd run over the object, whatever it was, that caused the flat. Nobody else could be blamed for this one.

While the kids formed a brigade to shift luggage far onto the grass away from the coach, Rafe heard a car in the distance coming down the road. He didn't have to guess that the smooth humming of the motor was a large, American-made sedan. It definitely wasn't one of the old trucks they'd heard going down this road all afternoon without stopping.

No, of course, it was a car. And as he expected, it turned in at the gates of Casa Esperanza. It stopped next to the bus and Carrie came out the passenger side. "Great. I thought you'd be halfway to the border without me by now. Thanks for waiting." She seemed confused by the laughter that rang around her. "Okay, somebody let me in on the joke."

Carrie felt really confused. She was quite happy, but truly confused. The last thing she expected was that Rafe and the kids would still be here, waiting for her. And why was everybody laughing? "Trent, explain this to me, will you?"

"I guess it's the power of prayer, Aunt Carrie. Rafe was sure we were going to be in Arizona before you showed up. But we didn't get to the front gate, thanks to something he ran over on the road."

Now she understood the laughter. It lifted her heart to know that nobody else wanted to leave without her. And she'd already told herself that Rafe had given up

213

on her, more or less, because of her decision to go to San Diego. Rafe was going to be mad, dealing with this miniature disaster. "How bad is the damage?"

Jake looked up from where he leaned over the wheel well. "They had started unloading the luggage compartments before you got here. This whole coach has to be empty to change the tire."

"And I'll bet you don't carry the kind of equipment to jack it up, either." The coach looked as difficult to switch tires on as a fire rig, and Carrie knew what a production that was. "Do you have a way to change it?"

"Jaime thinks he knows somebody who could do it. We may be here a while."

"Okay." Carrie realized suddenly that she'd just been taking this all in without sharing any of it with Dr. O'Connor or introducing him to anyone. She opened the car door and told him what was going on.

Watching him while he talked gave her a small shock. His resemblance to Rafe, not just physically, but the way they thought, was so unreal. That had taken her by surprise several times in the last few hours and it did again now. After hearing her explanation he rolled his eyes. "You mean an inanimate object dared to foul up the schedule? How could this be?" His eyes sparkled in a way that made Carrie want to laugh out loud, but she didn't want to wake Lucia in the back seat. The little girl had been through a long day, and she deserved the rest.

"I know. It won't make for the best circumstances to have any kind of civil discussion," Carrie told him.

Russ O'Connor became much more serious looking. "I'm not sure there are good circumstances for any of the discussions Rafe and I need to have, Carrie. Maybe this will turn out to be a blessing after all."

"If you say so." Carrie was still wondering how God could use this situation for their good. This day had been too wonderful already not to expect more miracles to come from it. She just didn't know yet how they would happen.

Russ pulled a cell phone out of his pocket and slid out of the car. He left the door open to spread the soft glow of the interior light. "For once, my obsession with work may pay off. I bet I know everybody in the medical or rescue field in the greater San Diego area, even this far south of the border. And I expect I can find somebody with the kind of pneumatic air bag you need to boost that coach off the ground in fifteen minutes or less."

"Fantastic." His movements reminded Carrie of Rafe, too. He was quick, but spare in motion, not wasting any effort. Except for his paler skin and the thick red hair going gray, Carrie could see before her a picture of Rafe in thirty years. It was an attractive picture.

Russ stood next to the open car door and made phone calls while Carrie went over to check on the human chain unloading the coach. She hugged Trent as best she could around the duffel bags he was shifting around, and went to find Rafe.

She found him standing away from the group, past the bus and away from the side of the road, just staring up at the star-filled sky. Carrie wasn't sure how to approach him without starting a huge argument. In the end she just took a deep breath and waded into the conversation. "Rafe? Please don't start yelling yet. If you want to yell, do it later. But for now, try to see this situation from my perspective for a minute or two."

He looked near the end of his rope. Dark hair stuck up in several directions where he had obviously been running his hand through it in frustration. "I would need a lot longer than a minute or two to see any of this from your perspective. It would take another lifetime, Carrie."

"Well, that's too bad, because we probably only have an hour or so before we can load this up and get going again. Your father thinks he knows who to contact to get the right kind of equipment here quickly."

"So it really is him in there."

"Yes. You expected that?"

"Once Rosa told me where you'd gone, I did. And he probably does know the right person to contact, too." Rafe's shoulders slumped. "He's probably glad to get me on my way as quickly as possible so we don't get into an argument."

Carrie refrained from laughing. "I don't think that's the case, Rafe. He's convinced that he's going with us, at least as far as Rob's place, once the coach is back together."

She didn't think Rafe could look more stunned. "This is like a nightmare. If anybody could have told me to dream up a worse situation, I wouldn't be able to do it."

"Hey, you're the Bible expert around

here. If anybody should know that God works in ways that pass our understanding, it ought to be you." Carrie had given up trying to figure it out herself. Today had been so wild, even by her own standards, that she was giddy.

"Are you sure about this? My father wants to go with us on the bus to Tulsa?" Rafe paled. "At least tell me that you're going, too. And you've convinced Lucia to stay here."

He looked so pathetic she wanted to hug him. "Yes, I'm going. And Lucia understands that I have to go away for a while. But that's part of what your dad wants to come with us and talk about. I think we worked out a way that I can come back here soon, to live. We need to talk about it on the way home."

She nearly took a step backward in surprise. "Wow, I just realized . . . Missouri won't be home for much longer, will it? If I move out here, I mean. I guess I better stop thinking about it that way."

Rafe looked at her. His mouth was hanging open just a little bit. "You think you've worked out a way to come back? Just like that? Do you realize what it means, quitting your job, finding one out here, a place, everything?"

"I'm beginning to. And I can hardly wait."

He was shaking his head now, and she could tell by his motions that he was ready to turn away from her. "I thought you were crazy, Carrie. Now I know for sure that you're totally certifiable." Without another word he walked away.

Carrie watched him go, knowing in her heart this time that her decision would cut Rafe out of her life as fast as he'd come into it such a short while ago. It hurt to the core of her being, but she knew this was right. This was what she had to do.

Chapter Fourteen

The bus was incredibly quiet. It was almost two in the morning, at least by the time zone they'd been in for a week, and one of Jake's gospel tapes was playing quietly over the speakers. The kids were so worn-out, they were all asleep. Carrie wished she could join them, but watching the men in the two front seats sit across from each other, each sitting straight upright and awake, yet silent, was taking all her attention.

She'd been watching those stiff-necked fools for almost an hour and neither of them had moved toward the other one. Rafe hadn't said much more to her, either, since they'd spoken at the bus hours ago. At least she knew who Rafe took after in the temperament department. Finally she went up to the seat behind Rafe, which was empty. The kids knew enough to give those two a wide berth once they all found out who the older man was. Carrie could tell, back at the children's home, that Rafe had tried to think of every way possible of denying his father access to the bus.

But there was no good reason for him not to go along, especially when Rafe knew his father would be even more welcome at Rob's for Easter Sunday than the busload of kids. His brother and sister were on good terms with his father, from what he'd said, and even Rafe couldn't find a reason to deny his father a ride that far if he wanted one.

If they were speaking to each other he would have loved to ask his dad a few pointed questions, like how he was getting back to Casa Esperanza from Rob's. Surely a methodical person like his father had that all worked out before he got on the bus. Rafe knew he would have, if it had been him. Of course, it would never have *been* him in this situation, because unlike Carrie and his father, he didn't make rash decisions like driving to Mexico and leaving his car someplace so he could hop on a bus and head for Tulsa, Oklahoma.

It was obvious from his behavior, though, that Rafe didn't have any intention of welcoming the man with open arms. If that was unexpected for Russ, he didn't show it. By the time the tire was changed and all the goodbyes said for the second time, Russ O'Connor climbed aboard the bus with everyone else, talking to the kids, and to Carrie, but not to his son.

They hadn't talked since. The coach full of people made the border crossing by ten-thirty and zipped down the freeways in the California darkness ever since. By the road signs, Carrie knew they were already in Arizona, and still those two were quiet as clams. This had to stop.

They both seemed startled when she sat behind Rafe, put her good hand on his shoulder and started talking. "All right, let's call this meeting to order. We can talk about something neutral for a while if you like, such as what Renata has planned for this crew when we get to her place. We can talk about baseball, or how long you two think I'm going to keep this cast on my arm, or the fact that nobody on the bus will ever take hot running water for granted again. But we're going to talk."

"Maybe you're going to talk —" Rafe didn't even turn toward her "— but I was railroaded into this."

"Like I wasn't?" His father at least sounded jovial. "You didn't have this wild woman park herself in your office and refuse to move until you came out."

"No, I only had to set her arm."

"Oh, you did no such thing. You just had to tell me I was going to get to wear a cast." At least the two of them were talking to each other. Carrie sent up little mini-prayers of blessing.

"And you took that news so well."

Russ laughed softly. "I'll bet she did. She scared my secretary witless, and Blanche doesn't scare easily."

Rafe finally turned toward his father. "Blanche is still working for you? How on earth do you keep her?"

"Being the obnoxious old coot I am? And don't say that wasn't what you were thinking. We may not have spoken recently but I still know you, Rafe, and that's what you were thinking. I keep Blanche with lots of benefits and even more prayer, because I don't deserve her. Just like I don't deserve this second chance with you, but thanks to this young woman I've gotten it."

Rafe made a wry face. "Telling the truth gets us both in trouble, doesn't it?"

"Ah, Rafe, if only you knew. The one regret I have in my whole relationship with you is telling you a lie."

His father's words were soft, and Rafe seemed riveted to him. It was the last thing Carrie had expected to hear from one of the upright O'Connor men. "What do you mean?" he asked.

"Just that. I lied to you once, and if I had it to do over again, I would never do it. Not even when it meant breaking a promise to your mother, God bless her."

"Only once? What about all those baseball games you never saw, and the programs at school Mom went to by herself?"

Russ slid to the edge of the seat. Carrie held her breath, feeling the air between the two men crackle with the feelings between them. "I meant to get there almost every time. Honestly, Rafe. I know I was a lousy father. But that isn't what I regret, because I probably wouldn't have been able to do anything any other way. What I regret is promising your mother after you were born that I'd never tell you how sick she was."

"You mean you knew? It was an ongoing problem from that far back?"

"From the day we met. Cruz had heart-valve problems from something she contracted in childhood. By the time I knew her, she'd decided she wasn't going to have the surgery to repair anything. It was too risky back then and she couldn't spare the time. I never saw anybody who treasured life and lived every moment of it like your mother, Rafe."

"Why did you let her —" Rafe seemed to grapple for words "— live the way she did? Why didn't you stop her, slow her down?"

"Like reminding her she was risking her life with the birth of every new child? Convincing her that staying with her sister for weeks at a time in rural Mexico wasn't a great idea? Telling her to slow down and conserve her energy so she might live long enough to see our kids grow up? Remember who we're talking about here."

Rafe leaned back against his seat. Carrie ached to reach out to him. She could see from his expression what revelations his father's words were causing. They made her own head spin, because they put everything Rafe had told her about his mother, and his father, in such a different light.

Russ reached over the seat and touched Rafe's shoulder. Carrie was gratified to see that he didn't flinch. "Son, you've devoted your life to being like your mother. At least you think you have. But you're my son, too. And I see so much of you in me."

"Now there's a scary prospect." Rafe's words were grimly quiet.

"In more ways than you can ever know. But it's true, Rafe. I see the disciplined, structured young man I was at thirty. In my case, I just got more that way as life went on and I compartmentalized all the things that bothered me about life. Don't do that, son. Don't shut out the world just because it hurts."

Rafe looked away from his father. "Carrie?" Russ calling her name startled her. She was so entranced listening to the two of them, she'd almost forgotten they knew she was there. "Do you love him? Do you love this stubborn, brilliant son of mine?"

"Yes, I do." Why didn't it surprise her to admit that? Maybe because she'd known it for some time. "I don't agree with him half the time. He's opinionated and blunt. Probably the most driven person I've met in years. But, yes, I do think I love him."

"Then try to explain to him what you want to do. Try to tell him why you do things the way you do. See if you can make him understand." There was a note of pleading in Russ's voice Carrie didn't think was possible. He was such a strong, assertive individual, it didn't seem likely that he'd ever pleaded for anything in his life.

"Oh, he understands what I want to do. He probably even understands the power of the Holy Spirit that allows me to do it. Listen, both of you, I know this isn't my doing. It's just that Rafe can look at all of this from a sane perspective. And he thinks I'm crazy for wanting to do it. Even though if there's anybody to blame in this world for what I'm going to do, it would have to be him."

"Oh, no. You can't hang this one on me. If you want to blame somebody, you can blame your volleyball team." Rafe sounded strained.

Carrie sighed. "I know nobody, including you, talked me into going to Mexico. Although my family did put a fair amount of pressure on me, no one made that decision but me. And I wouldn't have gone, probably, if I hadn't broken my wrist. But, Rafe, you showed me this whole new world. It touched me. It grabbed me and won't let me go. And now you expect me to pretend I've never seen it?"

"Not pretend you've never seen it." His voice was flat, and when Rafe turned around toward Carrie, his eyes were almost as flat. "Just react like a normal person for once in your life. Go back home, get your cast off and go back to work. Send a big chunk of your paycheck south to Rosa and Jaime, if you need to. Go down there when you can to visit. If you're sure it's the thing to do after a while, maybe even apply to adopt Lucia. Just don't go off on the first whim that stirs you."

"I think it's too late for that. I think it may have been too late for that the moment Lucia talked to me."

"Then I'm sorry, Carrie. Because you are going to have to do this without any help from me. If you do this thing, whatever was between us is over."

From the next seat over, Russ O'Connor sighed. "I'm sorry, too, son. Because if that's the case, you're more like me than I thought. And I think maybe we're both fools."

Renata seconded her father's opinion of Rafe. Rafe could see it in her eyes even before she said anything. While everyone from the bus was taking a shower, eating a hot meal or playing a rousing game of softball, Renata listened while he talked.

It probably took him half an hour to fill her in on the last five days. The first four days took about ten minutes, the last twenty-four hours the rest of the time. Even when he was done catching her up, Rafe had so many questions he didn't know where to begin. "Did you know about Mom?"

His sister seemed to be putting her

thoughts together in words he could understand. "Not in a conscious way. But I sensed something even when I was a teenager. Maybe it was a woman's kind of connection. But she looked at us sometimes, when she thought we weren't watching, in such a different way, Rafael."

He felt so dense while his sister described it. "How do you mean?"

"Hungry, somehow. Or longing. Like she knew she was only going to get so many birthdays and Christmases with us, and she wanted to store up each one." Renata choked up for a minute and Rafe felt like a heel putting his sister through this. "I guess when you think of it that way, she got quite a few, didn't she?"

"Not enough."

"No, perhaps not. Do any of us get enough? I don't think so. But hey, life's pretty good. Especially when you figure it's just the opening act before what Mama's already experiencing."

Renata's words hit him like a blow to the gut. As shocking as his sister's pronouncement of faith was, he knew she was right. Life *was* pretty good, and it would never be long enough to do all the things he wanted to do. Not if he continued to live in the same orderly, sane fashion as he was right now.

Maybe Carrie had a point with her lightning decisions. Maybe that's why this impulsive, impetuous woman had been brought into his life after all. Not to remind him of what he was already doing and doing well, but to challenge him to do even better. The thought was exhilarating and terrifying at the same time.

He felt like picking Renata up and whirling her around, like he had when they were kids. However, the sane, logical part of his mind that still held sway kept him from doing it, sheerly out of self-preservation. His sister wasn't a lithe nine-year-old anymore. She was a full-grown woman built similarly to his mother and aunt. If he didn't put his back out whirling her around, she'd playfully smack him into next week for doing it anyway.

"What would I do without you?" His question took Renata by surprise. She threw her head back and laughed.

"Right now, have a whopping big motel bill for all those kids' showers and all the barbecue they went through today. But I assume you mean that in a broader sense."

"I do." He had to hug her, and Renata returned the hug with full force. "Thanks for listening. And knocking some sense into me."

"Anytime, Rafe. You want some sense knocked into you, I'm your woman. At least until Carrie gets that cast off. Now, what are you going to do?"

"What the kids have been doing all along. Eat some of that barbecue, get a shower, then go back to being a grown-up and herd them all on the bus. And stay up all night talking to Papa."

"Cool. Can I warn Rob what's coming his way?"

"As long as you stick to general terms. I figure we've got about twelve hours on that bus to either bond or drive each other totally crazy. It could be either one by the time we get to Tulsa."

"That's my brother." She clapped him on the back in a playful fashion as they both headed toward the field where the barbecue and softball were set up. "Always the optimist."

"Hey, old habits are hard to break." He was going to try, though.

Carrie was so tired, she could hardly keep her eyes open, even to umpire the softball game. She couldn't believe how the kids could play with such energy.

The magnitude of what was facing her at home began to pile up like stones. Could she really do what she told Rafe she was going to accomplish? Just telling her family about these decisions was going to take more courage than she could muster right now. She could imagine her father's face when she broke the news that she was quitting her job and moving nearly two thousand miles away to help start a free clinic and adopt a child.

It was monumental, considering that five days ago none of this was even the vaguest possibility. Her family was used to wild spur-of-the-moment decisions on her part, but they usually involved tamer stuff, like trading in her car for a Jeep, or that time the Fire and Rescue guys had dared her to go bungee jumping with them.

How much of this would her dad try to talk her out of? And how much would she let him? She wasn't a child to be influenced. Still, she knew how happy Hank was to finally have all three of his daughters in the same place, at the same time again. How could she mess things up just when everybody else was happy in Friedens?

"Aunt Carrie? Was she safe or out?" Trent's impatient question from ten feet away where he was playing catcher broke through her mental fog.

"What do you think?" Carrie had no idea who "she" was, or what the play had involved. For once in her life she had been so deep in thought that the details of a sports incident had totally passed her by.

"I think we need a new ump." Trent didn't sound too put out. "This one needs some sleep."

Carrie couldn't argue. It would take at least twelve hours in a real bed, with lovely clean sheets, before she could answer any question coherently again. Even after that, she wasn't sure if most of her reasoning would make sense. But she was certainly ready to give it a chance and find out.

Not that the opportunity to rest in her own bed, without responsibilities, would present itself for a while. She was still one of the adults in charge of this crew and they were more than eight hundred miles from home. Her head hurt just thinking about it all.

"Twenty-minute warning!" Rafe's strident call cut through her exhaustion. He stood by the picnic tables Renata had set up, with a plate in his hand. And he looked calmer than Carrie had seen him in thirty-six hours.

That was a switch. She was getting more confused by the moment. Rafe looked like he could wrestle alligators all of a sudden. Just the contrast in their appearance made her heart sink. Who was this confident, handsome man and how could she have ever thought she was in love with him? Or that he could ever return her love?

Carrie kept herself upright long enough to help the kids gather the softball equipment and put it away for Renata. She was sure she told Rafe's sister thank-you for her hospitality, although she couldn't remember exactly what words she had used. Somehow she managed to get back on the bus, where Letty was preparing to drive into Texas on the next leg of the trip.

They hadn't gotten to the first highway exit before Carrie felt herself fading. And when she woke again, it was dark. The coach was stopped and the kids were milling around in the aisle.

She had no idea what day it was, what time zone, what state. Her mouth felt too dry to ask Trent or Heather or Ashleigh those things. When she could focus enough to read, she looked for some sign in the parking lot they were pulled into.

What she saw filled her with disbelief. They were back in Oklahoma at Rob's church. She'd been asleep for close to ten hours, through hundreds of miles of roads, several driver changes and a long night's vigil leading to Easter sunrise. Now they were here, and the sun seemed to glow over the horizon, promising that sunrise was coming up soon. But where were Rafe and his father?

They weren't in the first wave of kids she encountered in the parking lot after she stumbled off the bus. Nor were they anywhere in the mass of people in the gym offering the weary travelers food and a chance to clean up before services started. Carrie still felt wobbly on her feet as she surveyed all the people there.

Finally, in the corner, grasping a cup of coffee, she found Russ O'Connor. He and Rob were talking in an animated way. Both seemed happy. Rob didn't look very surprised to see his father, but then Carrie felt sure Renata had passed on the message of his father's arrival as quickly as she could.

"Okay, you two. What did you do with Rafe?" Carrie's throat felt tight, and her eyes still felt as if someone had thrown sand in them.

"Nothing." Russ was still smiling. "He passed up coffee for a chance to go in the sanctuary and pray before anybody else got in there. I might suggest you join him."

"I will." Carrie headed in that direction. She had never faced a church on Easter Sunday looking like she did, but then she'd never gone into a sanctuary on Easter *feeling* the way she did, either.

None of the lights were on in the big sanctuary. A few candles glimmered over banks of lilies heaped up all around the altar and in front of the first rows of pews. Way over to the side, Carrie saw one lone figure bowed over a bench, deep in thought or prayer. It was Rafe and she was drawn to him like a magnet. *Help me say the right thing,* she mentally whispered, unsure even as she prayed the words what that right thing would be when she got to Rafael's side.

Chapter Fifteen

Rafe looked up when Carrie got close to him. His expression was surprisingly calm and peaceful and his smile was fantastic. It made butterflies dance in her stomach. "Hi. Did you sleep well?"

"I feel like I got hit by a truck. Why didn't you wake me up?"

"Because you needed the rest. As your friend or your doctor, I wouldn't have woken you up for all the world. Besides, I spent the night talking to my father. I needed to do that as much as you needed to sleep."

"You don't look like a man who stayed up all night. Neither does he." Rafe looked absolutely perky, which added to Carrie's grumpiness and confusion.

"Well, if you don't mind me saying so, you don't look like somebody who's well rested and ready to face the day. And it's Easter, Carrie. What better day to begin a new life?"

"None, if you're really ready. Which is what I came in here for, Rafe. To tell you that you were right and I was wrong. I had to have been crazy to think I could just drop everything and start all over again across the country."

Rafe stood up quickly and took her in his arms. It felt so wonderful that Carrie forgot she had decided she didn't belong there, ever again. She didn't fight his embrace, or wonder if it was right or proper to let him hug her in church. "We seem to have gotten a point of view trans-fusion overnight and you got the worst of the deal," he commented.

"Oh?" She didn't feel capable of complex sentences right now with Rafe so close.

"Yeah. Your impulsive, positive behavior finally rubbed off on me. I didn't even stop the kids when they decorated Jeremy with shaving cream while he was asleep."

"You're kidding. That's awful."

"No, Carrie, don't you see? It's wonderful. I'm actually learning to let go a little. Of course, I did keep them from decorating you."

"Thanks heaps." Rafe's strange new attitude was winning her over. It was also making a tingle of hope replace the butterflies in her stomach.

"You're welcome. Now we just have to give you another transfusion of your own crazy behavior. Because now that I'm infected you're going to have to keep me company." He leaned his forehead against hers and Carrie could barely think, his touch felt so good. "So, what would you normally do in this situation, if I were the one telling you that life just wasn't going to work out according to plan?"

"Which plan? The one where we have some fluffy dreamworld and live happily ever after? Or the one that seemed possible yesterday, where I move to San Diego, start a new life and adopt Lucia, but don't see you anymore because you think I'm crazy?"

It was difficult to think about what she'd do. Making the thought process even more difficult was the fact that Rafe had obviously not gone straight into the sanctuary after all. He'd stopped somewhere long enough to shave. The smooth skin of his chin and cheek, smelling of lime-scented shaving cream, was enticing.

It was too enticing. She had to keep her wits about her. Carrie knew she had come into this sanctuary to do the right thing. Why wasn't Rafe helping her do it? "I don't know what to say or do anymore. I'm so confused." Carrie broke away from him and sat down.

"So am I. But for a change, being confused doesn't feel that bad. And I don't think I want to go with either of those plans you were talking about. For one, we're just not the fluffy-dreamworld kind of people, are we?"

Carrie felt that hope flutter begin to blossom in her heart in a most surprising way. "Not really. Does this mean that you don't think I'm crazy for wanting to start over?"

"Well, I wouldn't say that. It still sounds pretty crazy to me. But after talking all night with my dad, and praying a lot, and watching you sleep, somehow it seems crazy but possible. Would you do one thing with me?" Rafe's eyes were shining as he took her hand. "Will you try something and see how you feel afterward?"

"Maybe. Probably. What do you want?" The fog that had enveloped her just wasn't lifting.

"In a few minutes this place is going to be full of people. Some you know and some you don't. And they're all going to watch me rededicate myself to Christ, right there in the front of the church with my kid brother saying words over me."

Of all the things she expected, this wasn't among them. "You? I can't think of anybody I know with more dedication already."

Rafe shook his head. "No, Carrie, you're wrong. Maybe I looked dedicated. What I've really been is miserly."

"What do you mean?"

"All along I've been concerned about giving back only the best. I worked so hard making sure that I gave only the things I thought were the right, proper things back to God. I used so much of my time following the rules and working on the right behavior. Then you came into my life."

"And corrupted you for good?"

"Hardly. You're such a breath of fresh air, Carrie. And I fought the notion that maybe I was supposed to learn something from you. But I have."

"What? I've been a terrible influence, Rafe. I can't keep the kids in line. I can't even build a decent wall with one hand in a cast. I can't do anything right and you've pointed it out time and again."

"And I hope you'll forgive me for that. Because if I've learned anything in the last week, it's that doing things right is vastly overrated."

"That isn't something I ever thought I'd hear from you."

Rafe laughed. That made the blossom of hope in her heart bloom like a rose, unable to be denied now. "Stick around, Carrie, and you'll hear plenty of amazing things from me. At least I hope so. Anyway, I plan to rededicate my life to God's purpose for me. Now. Today. Will you go through this rededication with me?"

"Yes." It was the first thing she didn't have to think about in quite a while. "And then what?"

"And then we go from there. Moment by moment, day by day and see where God leads us. We don't just leap into anything, but we don't plan it to death, either. You game for that?" He took her hands, working around the cast. Rafe looked down at her casted hand then. "This thing is going to have to go soon. I want to hold hands with you without all this stuff in the way."

"I'm game for that. Both getting rid of the cast, and seeing what comes next with you by my side. If that's what you're asking for, Rafael."

"I am. And not a moment too soon, because here comes everybody else."

The sanctuary lights came on, and there

were musicians lining up to play glory to God on this Easter Sunday, and little kids leading their parents into the beautifully decorated space, and their own youth group kids bursting in, as well. "Are you going to have that crew come down to the altar and lay hands on us to bless us?" Carrie asked, eyeing them with a little suspicion.

"Them, my father, anybody who wants to come. Why?"

"Because Trent and Jeremy have funny looks on their faces. Be prepared for ice cubes down your neck, or worse."

"It will be a refreshing experience. Now smile and kiss me quick before they realize what's going on."

And she did, knowing that there would be plenty of other times that she wouldn't have to sneak in a quick kiss with Rafe. The fun was just beginning.

Epilogue

Friedens, Missouri
Six months later

Friedens Chapel had seen a lot of weddings. It had even seen a lot of Collins family weddings, but Carrie was sure this one would top the others.

Her father's wedding eighteen months ago had been cheerful and relatively calm. For Hank and Gloria, the excitement had come later with Hank's heart surgery and the explosion of grandchildren that seemed to follow their tying the knot.

For Laurel and Jesse, their wedding had been a joyous celebration of the love they had both found the second time around, and a celebration of Jesse's recent victory in the county sheriff's election.

Carrie was sure her wedding today was going to be every bit as cheerful as her father's and as joyous as Laurel's. But given the people involved in the preparation and execution of it all, it would be neither calm nor sedate.

"¿*Mami?* Is it time yet? Time to sprinkle?" Lucia ran up to her, frothy pink dress surrounding her, dark curls bouncing. The basket of rose petals she was supposed to "sprinkle" came perilously close to spilling in front of Carrie's satin pumps.

"Not quite yet, Luce. Soon, okay? *Diez minuto.*" Ten minutes was the longest time period her busy five-year-old could handle. That much parenting Carrie had learned quickly.

"Okay. Where's Daddy and *Papi?*" She craned her head around Carrie's white skirt, looking up the aisle of the church.

"Behind that door up there, remember? The music will play, then they'll come out in their fancy suits and line up, and you'll go sprinkling your rose petals." They had talked about it and practiced and rehearsed for what seemed like forever. Lucia loved it all.

Shredded tissue paper had replaced the rose petals and a plastic bucket the fancy white basket when they'd practiced in the apartment in San Diego that Carrie now shared with her new daughter, and Rafe would share with them after today. When

"Papi" O'Connor had watched Lucia's latest practice performance at the clinic, he'd nearly fallen over laughing, but hid his mirth from his granddaughter-to-be so as not to hurt her feelings.

"I see *Papi!*" Lucia crowed. "Is it time?"

"Almost. We have to wait for Tía Laurel." It was hard to have a matron of honor who had to settle a six-week-old baby before she could walk down the aisle. At least Susanna was an easy baby so far. Either Jeremy or Ashleigh could jiggle her in the front pew while her mom walked down the aisle. Carrie had a hunch that sometime during the ceremony her newest niece would be back in her mother's arms. That was, if her father didn't monopolize her. Jesse was so proud of his beautiful daughter that he carried her everywhere.

Carrie had given the gorgeous baby plenty of attention in the week she'd been home preparing for the wedding. It tickled her to see that Rafe had shown plenty of interest in the baby, as well. Susanna had proven a wonderful icebreaker at all the different events that brought the families together.

There was a rustling of fabric and Carrie's attendants came through the door in the back of the room together. Claire seemed the most unruffled by all the excitement. Laurel looked as composed as she ever looked these days with the addition of a newborn to the household. Renata looked smashing. The deep wine-colored sheaths fit all of them to perfection, bringing out different highlights in each. Renata flashed her a smile and Carrie was so glad, again, that she'd gotten another sister out of the blending of these families.

"See, I told you that was organ music," Renata said to Laurel. "You got me so engrossed in that beautiful daughter of yours that we almost both missed our cue."

"She is something else, isn't she? I hope she doesn't spit up on her brother."

Renata waved a hand in dismissal around her bright bouquet. "That perfect little angel baby? Not a chance." She leaned down to Lucia and stroked her cheek. "How about you, angel baby number two? You ready to go do the flower-petal thing?"

Lucia nodded solemnly. She still wasn't always used to attention. Sometimes when she got what she felt was too much of it, she got quiet. Carrie was noticing so much about her daughter every day. Right now her huge brown eyes held a note of fear along with a bit of excitement.

"Renata's right, Luce. It's time to go sprinkle those flowers. You ready?"

She nodded again, vigorously. "Great. Then go up to Daddy and *Papi* and we'll be behind you."

Carrie gave her slightly reluctant child a push in the right direction, marveling again at how many of those she herself had gotten from her heavenly Father in the last six months.

From the moment that she and Rafe had knelt together to rededicate themselves to God, life had been one long, crazy adventure. It didn't all move as fast as she'd originally planned, and she suspected most events had moved faster than Rafe ever expected.

The Cruz O'Connor Children's Clinic had seen quite a few patients in the weeks it had been open. With Russ's contacts in the medical community, all kinds of gently used equipment had come their way. Carrie had seen plenty of Rosa as she'd spirited her charges across the border by any means possible to get treatment when Rafe and Carrie couldn't steal away to Casa Esperanza.

It was there at the children's home, of course, that he proposed to her finally, and where she accepted. She didn't have the heart to keep him waiting on an answer for even a moment. Rosa had made them promise, on the spot, to videotape the entire wedding so that all the kids at Casa Esperanza could see it. And Carrie knew that once they flew west again there would be a second wedding reception there for them.

"Somehow I don't think this is the way you practiced it," Renata said, looking up the aisle and calling Carrie out of her reverie.

Lucia's performance was definitely different from their practices. Instead of walking sedately down the aisle with handfuls of petals drifting in the breeze behind her, she was being very deliberate. A fistful of petals got deposited next to each pew. Some got a firm pat from the chubby brown hand to make sure they stayed where she put them.

Carrie could hardly contain a riot of laughter. "What's Rafe doing?"

"Smiling, actually. And Dad's about to lose it. No, check that, Dad has lost it. Rafe is giving him 'The Look,' but it's not doing any good. If Rob cracks up along with him, we're in deep trouble."

"Rob has his game face on. He's ready to

marry us. He won't crack up on us, I'm sure." Carrie wasn't really all that sure, but she was trying to reassure herself. Her handsome soon-to-be brother-in-law could stay serious long enough to pronounce the vows over them, couldn't he?

"All right, what's my granddaughter doing?" Hank's voice close to her ear made Carrie feel much calmer. His hand curving around her arm steadied her like nothing else could. "She'll be fine up there, Mom. Not any more trouble than you ever were at that age."

"Gee, thanks. That reassures me a lot, Dad." Carrie had memories of family weddings. Fortunately no one had ever trusted her to be a flower girl. She probably would have brought her catcher's mitt down the aisle with her.

"Oh, no. Tell me she didn't really . . ." Carrie looked down the aisle, where Lucia pounded another fistful of petals into the carpet. Leaning far over, the hem of her daughter's frothy pink skirt belled up in back. It revealed that her little angel baby had substituted her soccer shoes for the sweet pink Mary Janes that were supposed to go with the dress.

"Takes after her mother," Hank murmured in her ear. "Bright little thing, too.

Already knows how to tie up those laces."

It was on the tip of her tongue for Carrie to tell her father otherwise. Lucia had mastered many things, but shoe tying was still a struggle. Then she looked up into her father's face, to see his mouth twitching and his eyes sparkling.

"You rat. You helped her, didn't you?"

"Of course not. I wouldn't do a thing like that right before my daughter's wedding. Not even if it was the same daughter that got all her nephews cracked up in the pew during *my* wedding last year. No sir, not me. I'm just your fine, upstanding father of the bride."

"Right, Dad." Carrie tried not to giggle. Renata was traveling down the aisle now behind Lucia. Claire was in place to begin her own walk after Renata, with Laurel bringing up the rear. All of them seemed to be having a little problem with composure, but Carrie was trying to overlook that.

"Did Rafe know about this?" She hoped her groom wasn't having a panic attack at the front of the church. Then an even wilder thought crossed her mind. "Or should I ask if he helped put her up to that?"

She looked up to where the O'Connor men stood together in the front of

Friedens Chapel. Their ties were straight, their shirt fronts crisp and they presented a picture of starched perfection until her gaze reached the floor.

Then she knew who had convinced Lucia to wear her soccer shoes, or at least who hadn't stopped her. Because Rafe, his father and Rob had all tossed her careful plans for their attire to the wind. The glossy dress shoes that went with the tuxes were probably in a heap somewhere in an office where they'd all dressed for the wedding. Instead, three well-polished, but well-loved pairs of ornate boots poked out from their sharply creased trouser legs.

"Tried to find Ron a pair to match, seeing as he's up there helping officiate," Hank said, referring to Friedens' senior pastor and his good friend. "He offered to wear his fishing waders, but I said that wasn't necessary."

"Thank you. At least some common sense prevailed." She didn't dare look down at her own father's feet. She knew without looking that he was wearing his boots with his tux, as well. Carrie leaned into her father's arm. "So, shall we do this?"

"My pleasure. If anybody had told me that within two years of doing this myself we'd see all three of you married, I would have never believed them."

"Me, neither, Dad. And I bet you wouldn't have expected the granddaughter count to have risen so fast, either."

"No, but it's a nice, familiar thing. I'm used to a houseful of girls, remember? Having three again is a nice thing. At least for the moment. You know that the boys are hoping you two get busy right away and give them another male cousin, don't you? They want to be ahead of the game."

In the second row of the crowded church, Carrie could see her youngest nephew, Kyle, clap a hand over his mouth to stifle a whoop when he saw Lucia's footwear. "They're ahead of the game already, Dad. I think we all are."

"I'll agree with you on that one, Carrie." And with one last squeeze of her arm, her father propelled her up the aisle, much as she'd sent Lucia off a few minutes earlier.

At the end of the aisle waited Rafe and the beginning of another brand-new adventure. *Thank you, Lord. I can hardly wait to see what it is this time,* she prayed silently. Suddenly she could see nothing in front of her but the glow of joy in Rafe's eyes. And she was coming closer to that joy with every step she took.

In a heartbeat she was at his side, and Hank was handing her off to Rafael. "Ready?" her handsome groom whispered, eyes still alight.

"Always," she told him, putting her hand in his. Rob began the service and nothing else mattered anymore, not the flower petals, the cowboy boots, nothing. She was here in front of God and the people she loved to join her life to this wonderful man. It wouldn't be a perfect life every moment, but she knew that together it would be the best life she could imagine.

Dear Friends in Christ,

Some authors look on doing research as the downside of writing fiction. But I've had many of my most interesting adventures while researching books. This book was no exception.

If you've never been physically involved in helping others for love of Jesus, I would highly recommend it. There's enough work to go around for everybody, from the highly qualified to those like me who can do only the basics, like pounding nails or using a paintbrush.

I am personally indebted to the patient souls who ran the "It's Your Serve" project in St. Louis, Missouri, where I was allowed to help with house repairs. The folks there put up with a great deal. I must thank Dave Bower of Team Casa de Dios in connection with Baja Christian Ministries. Not only does he have a great Web site, but he is incredibly patient with questions from novices.

Whatever your personal opportunity to serve God is, I hope Carrie and Rafe's story might have nudged you a little closer to making it reality.

Blessings,

Lynn Bulock